andy spearman

Endless thanks to Andrea Cascardi and Michelle Frey for their enthusiasm and belief. Thanks also to Rodman Pratt of Toronto.

THIS IS A BORZOI BOOK PUBLISHED BY ALFRED A. KNOPF

Published in the United States by Alfred A. Knopf, an imprint of Random House Children's Books, a division of Random House, Inc., New York, and simultaneously in Canada by Random House of Canada Limited, Toronto.
Distributed by Random House, Inc., New York.

KNOPF, BORZOI BOOKS, and the colophon are registered trademarks of Random House, Inc.
www.randomhouse.com/kids

Illustration & Photo Credits
David Birnbaum: p. 48
Michelle Birnbaum: p. 199 (right)
Getty Images: pp. 17, 29, 88
Karen Harmon: p. 103 (top)
Library of Congress: pp. 83, 127, 132
Cynthia Marfori: pp. 55, 119
NASA: p. 157
The Natural History Museum, London: p. 28
Gregory A. Nelson: p. 188
Melissa A. Nelson: pp. 75, 103 (bottom), 172
Picturequest: p. 89
Rodrigo A. Sánchez: p. 2
Nancy Siscoe: p. 184
The Tornado Project: p. 149
Bob van der Poel: p. 110
Zoe: p. 40

Library of Congress Cataloging-in-Publication Data
Spearman, Andy.
Barry, boyhound / by Andy Spearman. — 1st ed.
p. cm.
SUMMARY: To the confusion of his friends and family, Barry starts chasing squirrels, eating food off the floor, and otherwise acting like a canine after a flea bite turns his human brain into that of a dog.
ISBN 0-375-83264-5 (trade) — ISBN 0-375-93264-X (lib. bdg.)
[1. Fleas—Fiction. 2. Dogs—Fiction. 3. Humorous stories.] I. Title.
PZ7.S7384Bar 2005
[E]—dc22 2005044311

Printed in the United States of America
September 2005
10 9 8 7 6 5 4 3 2 1
First Edition

To Rigo, Josephine, and Lizzy

contents

illustrations

& tangents*

*_**TAN**-**jent**_ A tangent is a mathematical function ($\tan x = \sin x/\cos x$, of course), but it also means something that is "peripheral," a polite way to say "not very important."

Don't feel like you have to read this
whole story all at once.
You can read it in bits and pieces; it's
entirely up to you.

Just to let you know:
it's about a boy named Barry, and
then some stuff happens.
He turns into a boyhound.
He eats something kind of horrible.
His mom gets mad.
He loses his pants.
He does something kind of bad.
His mom gets mad.
His sister gets scared.
Then something really bad happens.
But everything ends up pretty okay.

That's about it, except for a couple of
fleas and an exploding raccoon.

dramatis personae*

CHARACTER	TYPE
Barry	Mammal
Flea One	Insect
Flea Two	Insect
The Brothers	Mammals
Exploding raccoon	Former mammal
Janey	Mammal
Mrs. Barry's Mom	Mammal
Worm	Annelid
I'm With Stupid	Mammal
Vladimir Guerrero	Mammal
Squashed frog	Former amphibian
Monica	Mammal
19 other squirrels	19 other mammals
Cat	Mammal
Pierre	Marionette
Partial Pierre	Partial marionette
Driver of car	Mammal
Nurse	Mammal

* ***DRAW*-mah-tiss per-*SOH*-nay** This is a fancy Latin way to say who the characters in a story or play are. Some people use this phrase because they think it makes them sound important. Other people—for example, William Shakespeare—use it because they *are* important.

One tiny bite

Shhh. Please be quiet. Barry is going to wake up any minute, and when he does, everything will be entirely different.

He really needs his rest right now.

You see, when Barry wakes up, he will be a dog. Barry has never been a dog before, and there will be so many smelly new things to do and eat. Some of them will be pretty awful. But we can't talk about stinky dog stuff just yet, because it hasn't actually happened just yet. I'm afraid you're going to have to wait a few pages. I do apologize.

What we *can* do, though, is listen to a miniature conversation taking place right now on Barry's head. No, not *in* his head, like you sometimes get when you have a fever and your dreams are weird, or if you're one of those people who hear voices out of nowhere, or if you're walking down the street listening to *American Idiot* on headphones.

No, this conversation is entirely not like that at all. This conversation is happening right now, right there, on top of his head, in the middle of an itchy brown thicket of Barry's hair.

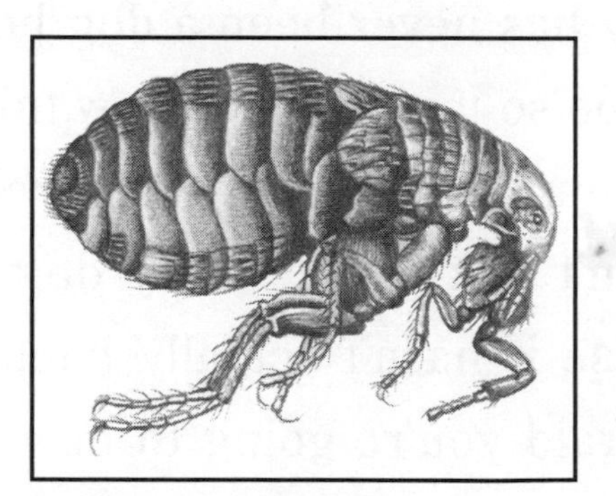

FLEE Look, fleas have no wings.

Up there on Barry's head

Flea One was the first to speak. That is why he is called Flea One. It is very logical. Otherwise he would be called Flea Two, and he would have to hold his tongue while the real Flea One spoke.

I know what you're thinking: fleas don't have tongues. Hey, it's just a figure of speech: "Hold your nozzle" doesn't have quite the same ring to it.

Oh, and fleas can't count to two? Don't be so difficult. Just listen to what these fleas have to say.

FLEA ONE: *Boy-o-boy, this is the life. Fresh blood, ya gotta love it. Ahh.*

Flea One leaned back on a large, comfortable flake of dandruff shaped exactly like the chairs dads sit in to watch the Super Bowl. There was plenty of dandruff to choose from up there on Barry's head, and Flea One sank his bony little body into the nicest, spongiest chunk: it was soft, yes, but with good back support.

Flea Two just kind of stood there, leaning on a hair.

FLEA TWO: *I'm tired of this racket. Get up, suck blood, hang around in the carpet, jump onto something else—it's the same thing every time.*

Flea One rolled his eyes and crossed a few of his legs. He'd heard it all before. Flea Two continued.

FLEA TWO: *I want wings. I want to fly. I want to be—*
FLEA ONE: *A mosquito. Yeah, yeah, yeah, you told me.*
FLEA TWO: *Being a flea sucks.*
FLEA ONE: *That's so funny I forgot to laugh.*

You just be quiet. I know fleas can't laugh. Or if they could, it certainly wouldn't be very loud. I bet it would be the tiniest tee-hee you ever did hear, *if* you ever did hear it, and I double dog doubt you ever did.

It's entirely safe to say that just about anybody could laugh louder than a flea.

But it's sad, because now Flea Two wandered off alone into an unknown region of Barry's scalp, feeling very sorry for himself.

He really did want to be a mosquito, but deep down in his little flea heart he knew he never could.

Flea One, on the other hand, was getting mighty hungry by now. He rolled off his dandruff recliner with a grunt and a yawn and a scratch, and probably another grunt, and found a nice plump reddish bit of Barry to bite.

Meanwhile

That was when Barry awoke, a boy no more.

HERE'S SOME STUFF YOU MIGHT WANT TO KNOW ABOUT FLEAS

1. There are over 2,000 different kinds of fleas in the world, but practically all fleas on cats and dogs are the same kind.
2. That flea is called the "cat flea." Strangely enough, even the fleas on dogs are cat fleas.
3. This way, dogs get to blame cats for all the fleas.
4. The average flea is about 3 millimeters long.
5. But boy, can they ever jump—up to 150 times their own length. That's sort of like you being able to jump 1,000 feet in the air.
6. Fleas usually live for only two to three months.
7. Sure, but a flea can lay 2,000 eggs in that time.
8. Fleas are ancient bugs, as old as dinosaurs.
9. And they're tropical, so they like the warm indoors.
10. Fleas can carry deadly diseases like the bubonic plague, which has killed hundreds of thousands of people.

A whole new dog

Barry was only twenty percent awake when he reached up and scratched the itchy spot behind his left ear.

Twenty percent was not quite awake enough to notice that he did not scratch the itch with his finger, as of course he normally did back when he was a boy.

No, he scratched the itch with the big toe of his left foot, as of course a dog normally does.

This is a kind of difficult thing to do unless you are in the circus and you practice a lot because it's your job and you get paid for it, or unless you are in fact a dog. Go ahead and try it. I'll wait down there, on the other side of these three little star thingies:

***

Told you. Now may we continue with the story?

***

Yawn, said Barry, who was now exactly fifty percent awake. Of course, he didn't actually say the word *yawn,* rhymes with *gone, prawn,* and *Kublai Khan.* What Barry actually said sounded more like *eeeeee-uhhmf-hoo,* which doesn't rhyme with anything except itself. But then neither do *purple, orange,* and *silver,* and those are actual real words.

Then he got up and went to the bathroom.

By this time Barry was about two-thirds awake, which was awake enough for him to notice that he was walking to the bathroom on all fours, on his hands and feet, like a dog.

KOO-blah KON Kublai Khan was a Mongol emperor who invaded China and created a city where Beijing is today. Marco Polo visited him and carried Chinese inventions like gunpowder, paper money, and sherbet back to Europe. But all the sherbet melted on the way.

That's funny, I'm walking like a dog, Barry thought to himself, not realizing how amazingly incredibly right he was. Although this did seem a bit strange to Barry, he also knew it was not wise to think too hard about stuff first thing in the morning, before you've had sugar.

On the bathroom floor Barry rolled over to take off his pajama bottoms, then rolled back again to lift up the toilet seat, then he cocked one leg into the air and started to—

—hold on a minute. Didn't anybody ever tell you it's not polite to watch somebody go to the bathroom? You should be ashamed of yourself.

Sheesh.

Even though he is now a dog, Barry would still like his privacy, thank you very much. So if you'll kindly close your eyes, plug your ears, and repeat the following rhyme nice and loud until Barry is finished. To be honest with you, it's a horrible little scrap of poetry about getting up in the morning, probably written by a boy.

Yawn, yawn
Go to the john
Or pee on the lawn
When your mother is gone

Oh. Sorry. Um, it looks like Barry is taking longer in the bathroom than I thought. A technical glitch, I guess you could call it. I'm not sure what he's doing in there, and honestly I'm not sure I would tell you even if I knew.

Let's go check on those fleas while we're waiting.

Up there on Barry's head

FLEA ONE: *Yodel-lay-hee-hoo! Where are you?*
FLEA TWO:
FLEA ONE: *I just want to talk to you. C'mon, buddy.*

There was no answer, even though Flea One spoke with his friendliest I'm-not-going-to-hurt-you voice. Flea Two wasn't going to fall for that old trick, or he had simply wandered too far away to hear.

Flea One was getting tired. And a bit angry. He had been waddling around Barry's scalp, calling and calling, but he was too full to go very far. You see, he had just been gorging himself on Barry's fresh warm blood, and now he felt as if he would burst at any moment, like a water balloon at a porcupine's pool party, and he had to sit down again.

Become a Poet Before You Know It

Making up poems is fun and easy.
In fact, it's easy peasy lemon squeezy.
Here's how to do it.

1. Write the alphabet across the top of a blank piece of paper.
2. Think of a word, then go through each letter and write down words that rhyme with it.
3. Think up a bunch more words to go in between until it all means something.

Meanwhile

After at least one million years, the toilet flushed.*

It's probably safe to go into the bathroom now, though you might want to hold your nose; it's entirely up to you.

Barry climbed up on top of the bathroom sink—he'd never done that before, honest—and took a good long look at himself in the mirror.

He squatted there and wondered.

He kind of sort of remembered one day long ago when he kind of sort of wished he could be a dog, because when you're a dog, you get to do everything and you don't have to do anything. But c'mon, it wasn't exactly up there in Barry's Top 3 Wishes. Top 10, yeah, okay. Top 5 at best. Come to think of it, maybe being a dog was in the Top 3 after all. But still,

***sir TOM-uss *KRA*-per** People like to say Sir Thomas Crapper invented the flush toilet. Sorry, but it just isn't true. He was in fact a plumber, and yes he invented some plumbing stuff. But somebody else was the first to figure out how to make poo go down a drain.

you'd think whoever's job it is to grant wishes would pay more attention.

***

Except that nobody wishes to be a boy-hound.

Nobody has to.

Wishing has nothing whatsoever to do with it.

***

Barry's true #1 Wish in life was to be big. Because when you're big, Barry thought, you're important, and when you're important, you get to be the boss, and when you're the boss, you know everything and you get to do whatever you want.

The only tricky part is deciding on all the stuff you might want to do when you're the boss. Barry figured he would just somehow automatically find out all that stuff when he became extremely big and old, like a teenager.

Perhaps, when the time comes, he will receive a pamphlet in the mail explaining everything:

DEAR BARRY, WELCOME TO BEING BIG!

This is going to be so cool.
Here is complete information on all the stuff you'll need to know starting today.

It would be pages and pages thick, and it would tell Barry how to deal with dumb boring old stuff, plus it would give him total info on neat new stuff, and it would be divided up into handy categories to make it easy to look stuff up:

ANNOYING THINGS
sisters, shoe polish, War of 1812, dental floss

COOL THINGS
nachos, staying up late, money, hockey equipment

EVIL THINGS
pimples, medicine, laundry, assembly instructions, salad

NEW THINGS
internal combustion engines,
power tools, drum kits

And so on.

That'll be useful, thought Barry.

***

He had been staring at himself in the mirror for a very long time. No matter how hard he looked, he looked exactly the same as always, except of course he was one day older than he was yesterday (and one day younger than he would be tomorrow), and if you looked closely, you could just about tell that he was also a fraction of a millimeter taller.

So yes, Barry was indeed exactly one teensy bit bigger today, and that made him exactly one teensy bit happier.

But there was more to it than that.

Oh yes. Much more.

Even though Barry looked pretty much the

same on the outside, he felt entirely different on the inside.

Somehow, overnight like magic, he had turned into a dog.

On the inside.

Not the outside.

It is important to remember that.

Yes, Barry had turned into a dog overnight like magic. A kind of hound. A *boyhound*. A very rare breed indeed.

BOY-hound A rare breed of animal that is a boy on the outside and a dog on the inside. Girlhounds also exist. Could happen overnight like magic or all of a sudden. Actual results may vary.

Sasquatch

If you have ever fallen from a helicopter onto a wedding cake, you'll know what an exploding raccoon is like. The raccoon exploded yesterday, before Barry turned into a boyhound overnight like magic, when he was out playing **Pirate** with his two best friends, the Brothers.

The **Compleat Pirate** rule book* states that one team draws a treasure map and the other team has to find the treasure before time runs out after the first team counts to 99 Mississippi to give a head start.

*See APPENDIX I if you want to read the **Compleat Pirate** rules and stuff.

The first team hides the treasure chest, actually an old tin box, which is dark green with a red cross on top, that the Brothers got from their garage.

You guessed it: the box used to be an army first-aid kit, and the Brothers said it was empty now since the bandages were all used up by soldiers who got shot, probably in the War of 1812, since the box was all old and dented.

Yesterday it was the Brothers' turn to hide the chest and draw the map and count the Mississippis. That was okay with Barry because the Brothers usually drew such good maps you'd swear they must have been actual pirates in a former life, before they moved in down the street from Barry.

Except they forgot one thing. On a map you pretty much have to put which way is north ↑ or else nobody will know which
N

way is up, especially not Barry.

This is how the map was supposed to look if you happened to know which way was north:

As with most school subjects, Barry didn't have much of a knack for geography. Even if you got grades for lunch, he'd lose marks for taking the tomato out of his sandwich.

I bet you already guessed: Barry held the map upside down, turning north into south and east into west, so on the next page is how it looked to him.

The Brothers were already counting . . . *14 Mississippi . . . 15 Mississippi* . . . so Barry charged off toward X MARKS THE SPOT, exactly in the entire wrong direction.

***

As a lot of lost people in this world can tell you, it's usually better to have no map at all than a wrong one.

See for yourself if you don't believe me:

Before we go any further, I have to tell you that the Brothers forgot to put north on the map entirely by accident. It was an oversight; normally the Brothers were sticklers for detail, as they say.

WHERE BARRY ACTUALLY WENT	**WHERE BARRY ACTUALLY SHOULD HAVE GONE**
Around Alligator Swamp, as everybody called it, except it was actually just a small marshy area with bulrushes and milkweeds where every mosquito on the entire planet comes from, especially when it starts to get dark out.	Under the three big willow trees.
Across the road without stopping and looking both ways.	Across the footbridge over the creek.
Across the railroad tracks, even though this is *EXTREMELY NOT ALLOWED!* according to everybody's mom. *She'll never find out,* thought Barry.	Over the fence.
To where X MARKS THE SPOT: the exploding raccoon.	To where X MARKS THE SPOT: the War of 1812 first-aid-kit treasure chest.

***

Barry was excited when he got to where X MARKS THE SPOT. Obviously he was way faster than the Brothers because they were nowhere in sight.

They're so dumb, thought Barry.

Barry had arrived at the edge of a gully

with a few low shrubs along the top. He double-checked the map—*yup!*—then folded it into his back pocket.

The **Compleat Pirate** states that when a player has found the treasure, he must yell the Official **Pirate** Yell in his loudest shiver-me-timbers voice—so if you're going to play **Pirate,** it may be a good idea to practice at home first, in a closet, for example, so as not to alarm pets or elderly guests.

The Official **Pirate** Yell goes like this:

Aaarrrrrrrgh!!!

I can't hear you. Try again:

Aaarrrrrrrgh!!!

There. Much better.

***

Barry took a deep breath. Then he yelled

Aaarrrrrrrgh!!! as loud as he could and took a running leap over a shrub and down into the gully.

At some point during the one or maybe two seconds he was in midair, Barry noticed there didn't seem to be any treasure at the bottom of the gully.

He got that right. Rather than the dark green War of 1812 first-aid-kit treasure chest indicated on Barry's map, lying there instead was a very large raccoon that happened to be dead at the time.

I'd have to ask a forensic pathologist* to be positive, but my guess is the raccoon had been dead, say, two days max—long enough that, yeah, it still looked pretty much like a raccoon, except under the hot sun all the gases and juices had been gurgling around

***fo-*REN*-zik pa-*THOL*-a-jist** Pathology is the science of disease and decay, and *forensic* simply means it has something to do with the law. So a forensic pathologist works in a lab to figure out how and when a victim died, but usually only for humans.

inside and now its body had puffed right up until it looked like a giant furry pan of Jiffy Pop.

But it was too late to turn back now. In the next half second or so, Barry landed right on top of it—

Splaaattt!!!

—and the raccoon exploded, spewing guts everywhere.

***

A useful reminder: it is extremely difficult to change directions in midair.

***

Barry was quite surprised at how loud and wet it sounded—like a whoopee cushion from *The Guinness Book of World Records* except, to say the least, a creamed raccoon has an incredibly putrid stench to go along with it.

***

As a general guide, not counting fish, the bigger the animal, the more rotten it smells when it's dead.

(Ants, by comparison, are virtually odorless.)

***

Then things got worse. As Barry sat there in a daze, smack in the middle of a spewed-out raccoon, he realized that the explosion had splattered him with hundreds of wiggly white maggots that now twitched all over his body like electric rice.

He jumped up in horror and shook himself in a frenzy, like Elvis Presley on fast-forward, batting the slimy bugs out of his hair and scraping them off his arms and scooping them out of his nose.

Then he rolled on the ground to smear any last stubborn maggots, turning himself into an instant Sasquatch as the loose dirt caked thickly onto his gut-soaked clothes. Finally, exhausted, he slowly skulked home, entirely unaware that maggots were not the only insects that had landed on top of him.

MAG-utz Maggots are the little wormy bugs called larvae (**LAR-vee**) that hatch after flies lay their eggs on dead animals or in a pile of rotting old disgusting garbage. Then, just as caterpillars turn into butterflies, maggots completely change—they grow wings and fly away to become . . . flies. This change is called metamorphosis (**met-a-MORE-fo-siss**). Maggots are picky and will only eat dead stuff, so they can't really hurt you. In fact, in the old gladiator days they plopped maggots right onto their wounds to heal them. Even today there are such things as "surgical maggots," which eat only the diseased parts of people's bodies. See your family doctor for details.

Up there on Barry's head

FLEA TWO: *Sheesh! What's all the racket?*
FLEA ONE: *Try to ignore it and get some shut-eye, pal. We've got a big day tomorrow.*

Meanwhile

The Brothers just kind of stood there next

SASS-kwatch Sasquatch is a dirty, shaggy half-man, half-beast creature who is said to roam the mountain forests of British Columbia, scaring campers and deer. But Sasquatch is "mythical," a polite way of saying totally fake.

to the treasure chest, exactly where the map said it would be if you so happened to know which way was north.

"What's *taking* him?" said a Brother, thrusting his hands deeply into his pockets.

4

How to be a boyhound

It's kind of a secret what Barry was doing for so long in the bathroom, but okay, maybe I can tell you if you promise not to tell anyone else.

Promise?

***

Okay.

***

Pinky swear?

***

Okay.

***

Cross your heart and hope to die?

***

Okay.

***

Stick a needle in your eye?

***

Okay, okay. I have to be sure I can trust you.

Crouching naked up on the sink, Barry noticed how sharply he could smell things this particular morning: the damp towel, the toilet, the drifting odor of his own body. He squatted there enjoying it quietly for a moment, then he gazed at himself in the mirror with droopy eyes and said, “Ah, that smells good.”

Except it actually came out as *Arf, woof grrrd.*

Barry jumped a little in surprise. He wasn’t prepared for that. He tried to speak English again:

Arf, woof grrrd, was all he could say to his puzzled reflection, and he jumped again and fell off the sink entirely.

Barry lay crumpled on the cold, moist bathroom floor. He could hardly believe what was happening to him—what in fact had already happened overnight like magic.

***

No points for guessing: turning into a boy-hound overnight was not the first possibility that crossed Barry's mind. It never is. But like everyone else this has happened to, he couldn't think of any other good explanation either. That's because there isn't one.

***

Moist, crumpled Barry did some thinking. He figured that turning into a dog was going to be either

A. One of the worst things that has ever happened, or
B. So cool

Barry had seen those werewolf movies where upon a full moon they sprout fur all over their bodies and grow fangs and attack

The Worst Things That Have Ever Happened to Me So Far

by

Barry

1. Peeing in my snowsuit.

2. Having a sister.

3. Eating raisins and finding out later they weren't raisins.

4. Going to the dentist.

5. Getting the blame for Grandma's silent farts.

everybody for no good reason. Barry glanced at his knuckles: they were still smooth.

Phew.

A useful reminder: even when there is only a small chance of becoming a werewolf, keep your eyes peeled just the same.

Slowly, cautiously, Barry lifted himself from the floor, rising up as if he were riding a creaky old elevator.* The top of his bed-head morning hair was the first thing to appear in the mirror, then his eyebrows, eyes, nose, and mouth.

The creaky old elevator, so to speak, came to a halt. Barry stood looking at himself: he still looked like himself. So he decided to experiment.

He tried to lick his own nose, but he couldn't quite reach, and gob dribbled down his chin. Oh well, nice try; he was new at this.

***ee-*LIE*-sha *OH*-tiss** Elisha Otis developed the first passenger elevator in 1857. Thanks to him, nobody has to take the stairs anymore.

He licked under his arm. There, much easier. And tastier too—with more salty flavor and a delicate hint of vinegar.

He pinched out a small fart: it wafted; he nodded.

He glanced at the toilet, but he just wasn't thirsty right now.

Barry thought that if there were this many great new boyhound things to do all by himself in a bathroom, just wait till he got to go outside.

***

Yup, Barry chose B. So cool.

***

Barry's eyes widened and a wicked grin spread across his face. "Cool!" he tried to shout, except of course it sounded more like *Ow-oooool!*

Plus it was really loud: ***Ow-oooool!***

"What was *that*!" he heard his little sister, Janey, say from downstairs.

Oops.

"I don't know . . ." His mom's soft voice carried easily up through the floor. Boy, was Barry's hearing good today.

"It's Barry. What a gomer," said Janey, not that you need special dog ears to hear her most of the time.

"Janey," said Mrs. Barry's Mom, and I bet she gave Janey a silent look. Then she called, "Barry! Breakfast!"

***

Just to let you know: Barry was pretty positive he would get into big trouble for turning into a boyhound, that his parents would totally wig out, even though it was kind of like catching measles or getting hit by a meteor. It generally isn't your fault.

But his mother might not see it that way. And if she found out the truth, then his father was *sure* to find out, and his father *definitely* would not see it that way. Mr. Barry's Dad had already made it "perfectly clear" on "a number of occasions" that he had had "quite enough" of Barry's "nonsense" and "tomfoolery," "thank you very much," unless Barry "really wanted" to be grounded "forever."

As Barry can tell you from the time he

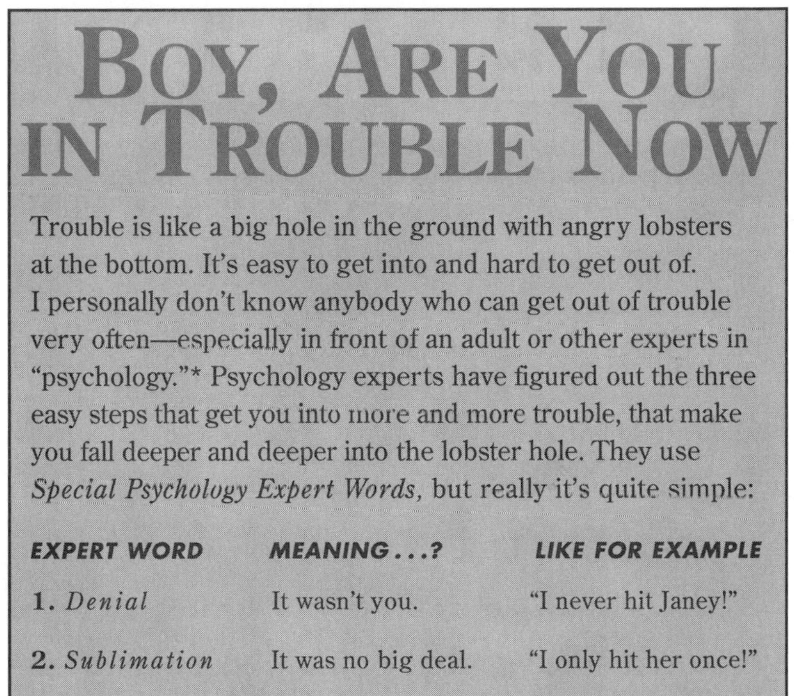

Boy, Are You in Trouble Now

Trouble is like a big hole in the ground with angry lobsters at the bottom. It's easy to get into and hard to get out of. I personally don't know anybody who can get out of trouble very often—especially in front of an adult or other experts in "psychology."* Psychology experts have figured out the three easy steps that get you into more and more trouble, that make you fall deeper and deeper into the lobster hole. They use *Special Psychology Expert Words,* but really it's quite simple:

EXPERT WORD	MEANING...?	LIKE FOR EXAMPLE
1. *Denial*	It wasn't you.	"I never hit Janey!"
2. *Sublimation*	It was no big deal.	"I only hit her once!"
3. *Projection*	It wasn't your fault.	"But she hit me first!"

***sy-*KOL*-lo-jee** Psychology is when people do a bunch of tests and then make a guess—called a "theory"—about what the heck is going on in people's big human brains.

spray-painted the car orange, "forever" could last for weeks.

So Barry had to pretend that he had not actually turned into a boyhound overnight like magic. It wasn't going to be easy—at first anyway, because

A. He had to remember to walk on only two legs.
B. He had to keep his mouth closed and not stand there with his tongue hanging out or lick his own nose.
C. He had to pretend that he didn't really want to go up and smell everything, especially things that are really, really smelly in the first place, like cheese in the back of the fridge and some people's breath in the morning.

That reminds me: if dogs have such a good sense of smell, how come they always have to get so close to stuff to smell it? I mean, for example, I can personally smell barf a mile away, easy. But can a dog? No, a dog has to go right up and stick his nose in the barf for like a whole hour and it never makes him throw up even once.

Maybe it so happens that dogs actually like the smell of barf. You never know.

Up there on Barry's head

FLEA ONE: *Are you crazy? Come down from there!*
FLEA TWO: *No.*
FLEA ONE: *Please?*
FLEA TWO: *No.*
FLEA ONE: *Pretty please with dandruff on top?*
FLEA TWO: *No.*

Flea One looked up at Flea Two—he *glared* at Flea Two. He was tired of arguing. Flea Two was also tired of arguing and looked far into the distance, pretending to scan the horizon for an approaching alien invasion or possibly the Spanish armada. He was wishing that Flea One would just please go away.

But if you want to know the truth, he was *secretly* wishing that Flea One would please climb up and save him.

***

Just to let you know: Flea Two was not a brave bug; he was really more of a chicken. I made him a bug in this story because a chicken is much too large to hide on your head unless you have maybe giant bingo hair. If you walked around with a chicken on your head, everybody would go "Hey, there's a chicken on your head," and then you'd have to think up an answer like "Yeah, so?"

TUNG A dog's tongue does a lot of work. It's how a dog eats and drinks of course. Also, a dog keeps cool by hanging his tongue out and panting. And he'll lick you if he likes you or whenever there's beef jerky under your fingernails.

***

So there was Flea Two, clinging in fear to the top of one of Barry's hairs, boinging back and forth, almost falling off every time Barry moved. He had shinnied up there earlier, and now he was being a complete chicken and not very much of a bug at all.

Meanwhile

Mrs. Barry's Mom hollered again: "Barry! You'll be late for school!"

Barry flushed the toilet again in case Janey or other spies were listening outside the door and got suspicious. Then he put on his baggiest pants and his baggiest sweatshirt in case he started to grow fur and paws and werewolf stuff in the middle of math class and needed a handy disguise.

He headed down the stairs very, very carefully, on two legs, very, very much like a boy, holding on tight to the banister the whole way.

And with each step Barry felt less and less like a boy and more and more entirely like a dog.

5

The horrible thing Barry ate for breakfast

Barry made it down all the stairs just like a boy, and you would hardly have noticed that he had in fact turned into a boyhound unless you could see inside his brain. Then you'd know that it was entirely different in there and that he was now in fact a dog.

***

That's the thing with your brain: it tells you how to think and act and feel, so it's a good idea to keep the wrong stuff from getting in there.

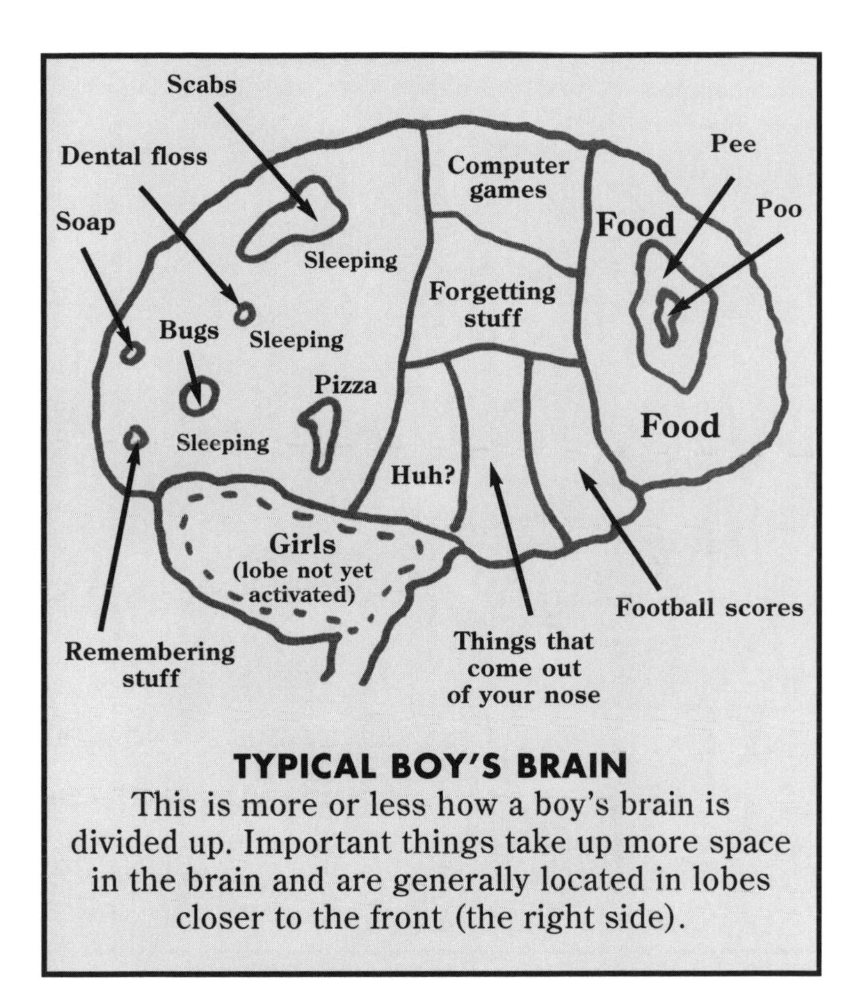

TYPICAL BOY'S BRAIN

This is more or less how a boy's brain is divided up. Important things take up more space in the brain and are generally located in lobes closer to the front (the right side).

***

Barry stepped carefully into the kitchen. His mom was standing by the back door helping Janey put on her knapsack.

"Good morning, sleepynoggin," said Mrs.

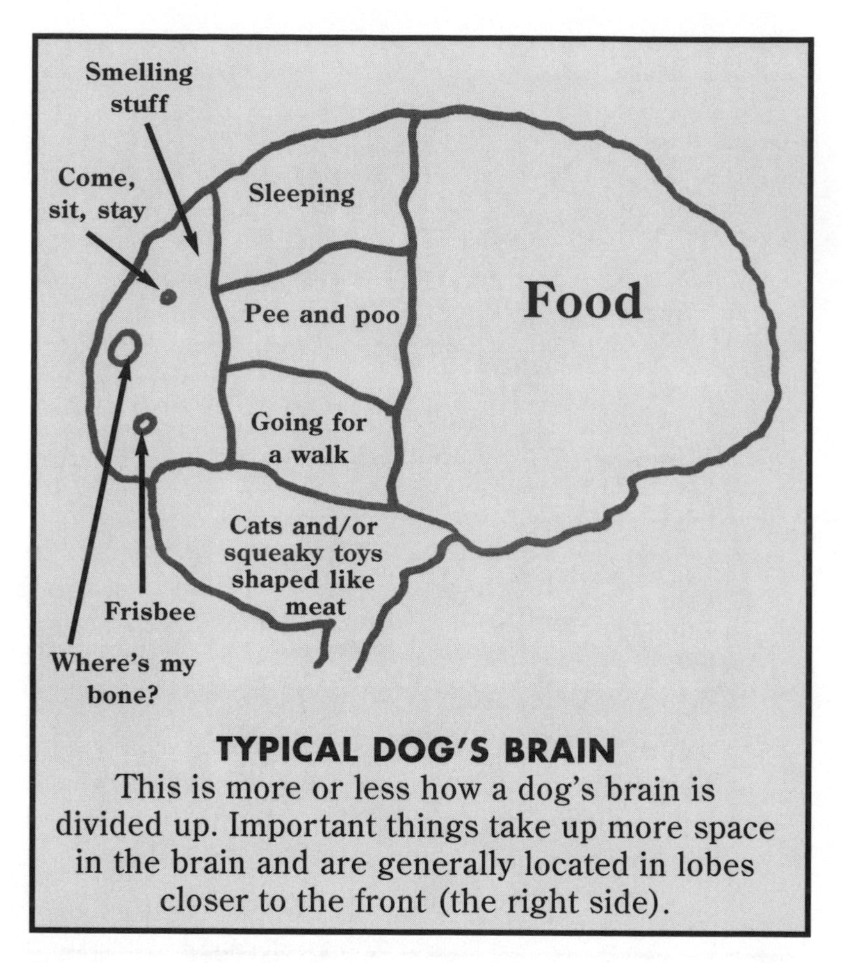

TYPICAL DOG'S BRAIN

This is more or less how a dog's brain is divided up. Important things take up more space in the brain and are generally located in lobes closer to the front (the right side).

Barry's Mom with a smile, which quickly turned into a scowl. "Oh, Barry, do you *have* to wear those pants?" And then simply, "Your hair."

Janey stood there, annoyed. "Oh, great.

You're late and now I have to walk to school with Jennifer Schmennifer. Thanks a *lot,* Barry Barely Barenaked Barry, remind me to send you a thank-you gift."

Barry narrowed his eyes and growled at Janey, and she slammed the door on the way out just as Mrs. Barry's Mom was saying something about holding hands crossing the road and blah blah blah.

***

For your information: Barry has growled at Janey plenty of times before, so it was no big deal on this particular occasion. Nobody suspected a thing.

***

Mrs. Barry's Mom took a deep breath to *collect herself,* as moms do.

Barry sat at the table and his mom asked, "What would you like for breakfast?"

Woof, said Barry. He didn't mean to say that.

His mom just laughed. "Waffles!" She was such a nice lady. "We only have waffles on Sundays, you silly mooncalf,* you know that. How about some cereal and orange juice?"

Arf, said Barry. Boy, was he nervous. Mrs. Barry's Mom looked puzzled. "Half? Half what? Oh, you mean half a glass of orange juice? Sure."

Yelp, said Barry. He honestly couldn't stop himself.

"Of course I can help. I'll get it for you. Poor thing—you look like you haven't slept a wink all night."

Ruff, said Barry.

"I'm sure it was," she said.

Anyway, they talked like that for a good minute or so and Barry was pretty positive his mom never once figured out that he had turned into a boyhound overnight like magic

***MOON-kaff** Someone who's as silly as a young cow on the moon.

and now absolutely everything was entirely different. He was lucky. A lucky dog. A lucky boyhound.

***

Until.

"Here's your cereal, sweetie." Mrs. Barry's Mom set the bowl down in front of him, then left the room to go do a bunch of mom stuff.

The floaty things in the bowl looked kind of familiar to Barry: crunchy-looking yellowy nuggets—

Let me guess, cereal? thought Barry, whose dog brain hadn't yet totally taken over his boy brain.

—and the crunchy-looking yellowy nuggets were bobbing around in some sort of cold wet white stuff—

Milk? Oh yeah, milk for sure; I bet it's milk.

Just to be positive, Barry leaned really, really far over the bowl until the tip of his nose just touched a crunchy-looking yellowy nugget, and that's when he found out it was also a very tickly yellowy nugget.

Snarfle! sneezed Barry.

The sneeze shook his head so hard that the bowl went flying, the crunchy-looking yellowy nuggets went flying, and the cold wet white stuff went flying as well.

It all went flying in all directions.

Mostly it went flying in the direction of the floor.

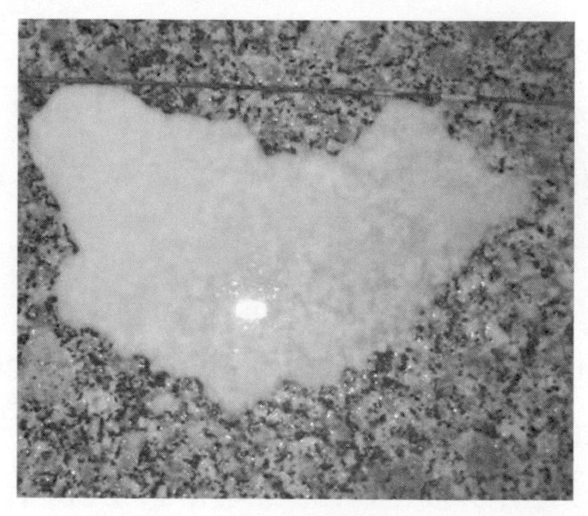

MILK Did you know that dogs are color-blind? This is what spilt milk looks like to them.

Up there on Barry's head

Fleas are like people. This is what they say when they're mad and they aren't talking to each other:

FLEA ONE:
FLEA TWO:
FLEA ONE:
FLEA TWO:
FLEA ONE:
FLEA TWO:
FLEA ONE:
FLEA TWO:

And so on.

Meanwhile

What a mess. Cereal was everywhere. Milk was even more everywhere. It dripped and splattered and smeared and went everywhere.

But to Barry, the breakfast looked even more delicious this way.

To Barry it was as lovely as a poem.

***

You probably don't need me to tell you: dogs have an entirely different way of looking at things.

***

A Dog's Breakfast

Milk

Is a pure white sea

Whose silent

Smooth

Surface

Is sailed by scattered ships of

Cereal

If dogs wrote about beautiful things, they'd write about food that has fallen on the floor. This poem is a metaphor (***MET-a-for***); it pretends that milk is a sea and bits of cereal are tiny ships that sail on it, but everybody knows it isn't true. It doesn't rhyme either.

Without thinking, Barry dove under the table, got on his elbows and knees, and slurped the milk up off the floor. (For someone who was a brand-new boyhound, Barry was surprisingly expert at this already.) He slurped up the cereal too, nugget after nugget.

Along the way he slurped up a number of other things that also happened to be under there at the time:

1. Hairs: a minimum of four
2. Elastic bands: one-half
3. Dried splotches of spaghetti sauce: two
4. Money: 1¢
5. LEGO: one policeman's torso
6. Spongy brown lumps, possibly toast, Styrofoam, or meatball substance: three

Barry was slurping his way under the table from one end to the other when his nose bumped into something. A boot. Somebody's boot lay on its side by the back door, caked with mud that oozed like melting butterscotch ice cream into the gray plastic boot tray.

That's when he saw the worm, working its way through the squelchy boot mud like an escape artist wriggling out of a strait-jacket.*

Barry sidled up closer. A quarter of an inch away.

FAIR WARNING

THE STORY MIGHT GET A BIT GROSS NOW, SO IF YOU WANT TO KEEP READING, IT'S ENTIRELY UP TO YOU

He sniffed.

Mmmmm, thought Barry, who was rather keen to explore this brave new world of taste sensations.

First—as a test—he carefully licked the worm.

Mmm, not bad, he decided. So he slurped

*__*HARE*-ee hoo-*DEE*-nee__* Harry Houdini was a famous escape artist from Hungary. He could escape from straitjackets, chains, jails, and even his special Upside-Down Water Torture Cell. But he couldn't escape from death; he died on Halloween 1926.

up the big fat slimy juicy noodley brown worm.

He got it halfway into his mouth, when he suddenly heard a voice from behind him.

"Barry?"

It was his mom.

Oh no.

She'd come back.

"Barry? Sweetie? Where are you?"

Barry immediately stood up and spun around. He stood there as still as a statue, frozen as a fish stick, scared as a squirrel at a square dance.

He was *petrified,* as they say.

The worm was half dangling out of his mouth, wagging sadly back and forth like it was on the dock waving bon voyage to the *Titanic,** somehow knowing something bad was destined to happen.

*__ty-TAN-ik__ *Titanic* was the largest ocean liner of its day, and people said it could never sink. So of course that's exactly what happened the very first time it ever went to sea. It hit an iceberg and sank in 1912.

Yup—she saw it. Couldn't miss it, really.

"Sweetie, are you okay?"

Barry slurped it all the way in and swallowed.

"Barry!" screamed Mrs. Barry's Mom.

What You Should Know Before Eating Any Worms

1. They don't actually taste good.
2. You can catch a disease and miss a lot of school.
3. Avoid the ones with legs. They are not worms; they are centipedes and they are poisonous—I'm serious.
4. Even if you wash them first, remember, worms eat dirt, so they're gritty in the middle. Avoid chewing.
5. Sun-dried worms have a somewhat nuttier flavor and a rubbery booger-like texture.

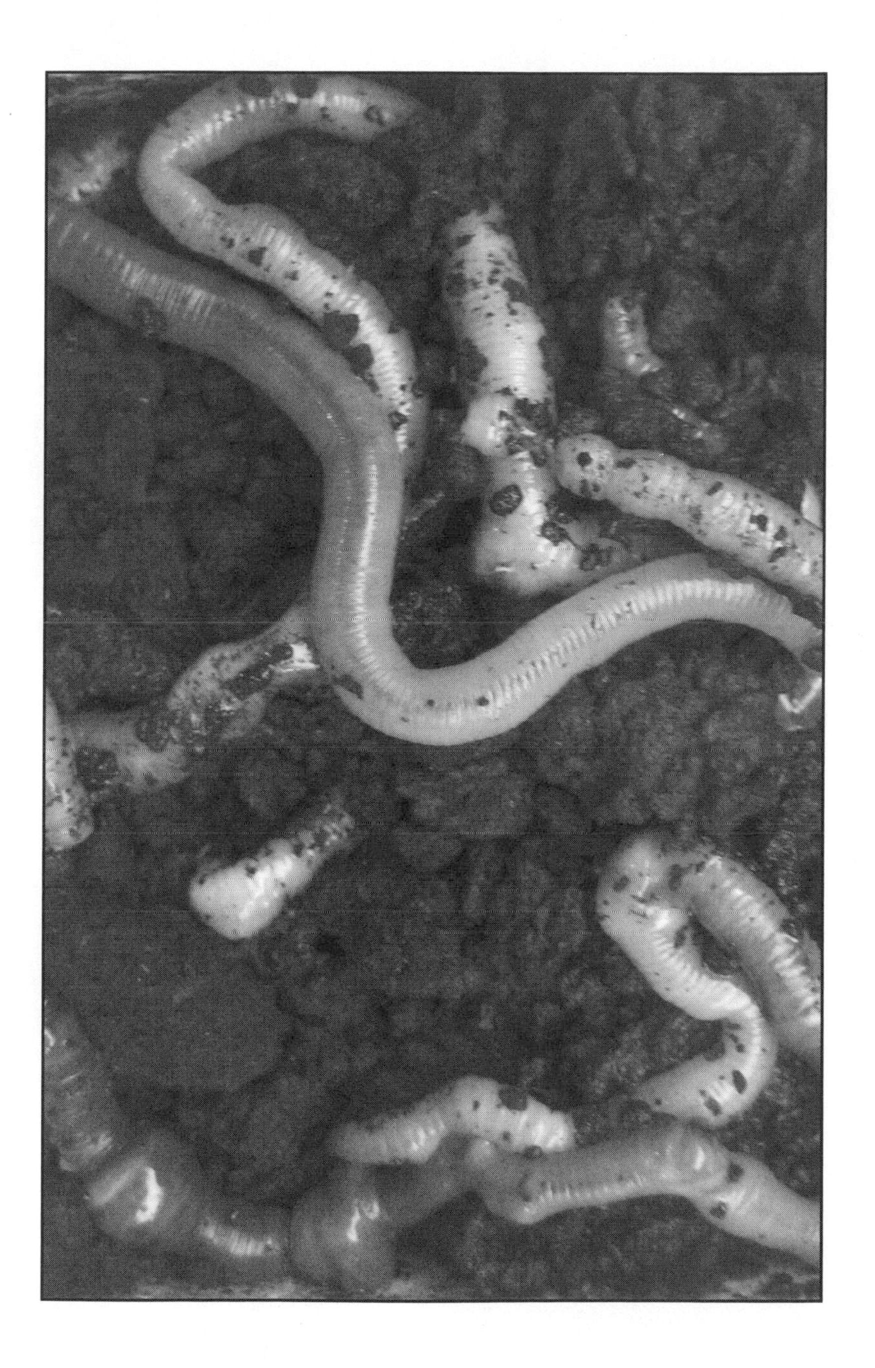

A note

Listen: I get the feeling that some weird dog stuff is about to happen to Barry, and I need to save up my energy. So I'm going to go have a little snooze now, and while I'm gone Mrs. Barry's Mom would like to say something. I have no idea what she wants to talk about, but she seems like a nice lady, so please sit up straight, listen with both ears, no talking, no snoring, and no picking your nose unless you're absolutely positive nobody can see.

Thank you.

*Hello, I am Barry's mother.
That's a lovely top you're
wearing. Do you know Barry?
He's been acting very
strange lately.
Yesterday he came home
smelling like a dead
raccoon, and today he is
behaving very badly.
Please let me know if you can
think of any reason for it.
Well, it was very nice to meet
you, except I wish
you would please stop
picking your nose.*

7

I'm With Stupid's dog

Mrs. Barry's Mom pressed her palm to Barry's forehead to see if Barry felt okay.

At times like this, some moms also want to take a gander at your tongue to make sure it hasn't turned purple or gone all furry. But since he just had a worm in his mouth, Mrs. Barry's Mom didn't want to get grossed out so early in the morning unless it was an actual emergency.

Instead, she looked at Barry for a minute, and Barry looked at the floor, where soggy ships of cereal slowly sank in the spreading sea of milk.

Mrs. Barry's Mom shook her head. She had no idea what could be wrong with Barry, if anything.

Well, actually, Mrs. Barry's Mom did have one idea, one psychology theory, which was often the correct one: that Barry was just being a schnook.

She put her hands on her hips and leaned forward, which any dog can tell you is a sure sign that a human is about to get mad and start hollering.

"Barry, you always act up when your father is away! You'd better smarten up before he comes back tomorrow! I'm warning you!"

Then she turned away and said, "Now go to school. It's late. There are two plain peanut butter sandwiches in your knapsack." Then she added one more thing that always annoyed Barry. "Hippity-hop," she said.

***

On the way to school Barry had plenty of time to think about this being-a-boyhound business. In his mind he came up with a whole list of good things about being a dog.

GOOD POINTS ABOUT BEING A DOG

1. Get to pee anywhere.
2. Get to eat with just your face.
3. Get to stay wet.
4. Get to hang your head out the car window.
5. Get to sleep naked anywhere, anytime.

Then he came up with another list of all the good things about not being a boy anymore:

GOOD POINTS ABOUT NOT BEING A BOY

1. No homework.
2. No snowpants.
3. No cleaning up your room.
4. No gagging on broccoli.
5. No dental floss.

The lists were actually quite a bit longer—178 points altogether if you must know. These are just the Top 5 to give you some idea.

To be fair, Barry also tried to come up with an equal list of bad points, but he couldn't think of any.

Up there on Barry's head

Still:

FLEA ONE:
FLEA TWO:
FLEA ONE:
FLEA TWO:
FLEA ONE:
FLEA TWO:
FLEA ONE:
FLEA TWO:

When fleas aren't talking to each other, it usually means they actually have an awful *lot* to say to each other. Maybe fleas ought to talk to each other more when they aren't talking to each other.

Dogs are entirely not like that. When a dog has something to say, he comes right out and says it. He says it if he hates you and he says it if he loves you and he says it everywhere in between. The thing is, dogs get all slobbery about it and they make you smell their pooey dog breath.

Meanwhile

Barry had been walking, lost in thought and lost in list making, for nearly an hour when he finally realized it only takes eight minutes to walk to school, or three minutes when he's forced to walk with Janey.

He looked up and noticed he wasn't anywhere near the school. He was in fact down by the big lake—I'm thinking, for example, Lake Erie—a place they only ever drove to in the car on Sundays to hunt for fossils, then maybe to buy something from the guy in the French fry truck.

Barry walked slowly toward the shore.

Slowly, because Barry could only stumble his way across the clumpy mounds of grass and sunken pockets of quaggy sand, like he was searching for peanuts in a pumpkin patch.

And because he had no clue how the heck he wound up here on the Dumbest Beach in the World in the first place.

Next to the water stood a man with hockey hair* in a red flannel shirt that was unbut-

****HAH*-kee hare** Hockey hair, also called a "mullet," is short on top and long at the back. One man, two haircuts. This style is still popular today with members of Canadian power-rock trios.

toned and flapping open so you could see his T-shirt beneath, which said:

I'M WITH STUPID

Under that was a hand that looked like:

☛

At this particular moment, the finger pointed way off into the distance toward an old lady minding her own beeswax and feeding a bag of bread crusts to some ducks.

***

Next time you see a guy wearing one of those T-shirts, you have my permission to go up and say "Hey, you borrow that from your girlfriend?" Then run real fast before he has time to figure out that he's been insulted.

***

I'm With Stupid threw a tennis ball into the lake, then suddenly out of nowhere a big dog—one of those lanky standard poodles without pink ribbons that you don't see much—crashed into the water, splashed out to the ball, and paddled back with it in his mouth like this was the easiest thing in the world.

"Atta boy, Vladdy," said I'm With Stupid, and he threw the ball even farther this time.

Barry watched them do this over and over again. It was exciting and boring at the same time, like when you're in a long line for the Tilt-A-Whirl and you have to stand there and watch other people ride a million times before it's finally your turn.

After a while I'm With Stupid went and sat on a rock and opened a can of root beer or something, his T-shirt now accusing an innocent jogger.

The dog still stood there, the ball dripping in his mouth. The dog looked at Barry. Barry looked at the dog. They stepped toward each

How to Pick a Poodle

Poodles come in three handy sizes to suit all your poodle needs: toy (really small), miniature (small), and standard (actually fairly big). Review the list below to choose the poodle that's right for you.

	Toy	Miniature	Standard
It's okay to tie pink ribbons in its fur.	✔	✔	
It's okay to make it wear a cute little jacket when it starts to get chilly out.	✔	✔	
Females have exotic French names like Fifi, Mimi, and Dominique.	✔	✔	
Males have tough-guy names like Jean Reno and Napoleon.			✔
Its haircuts cost more than your mom's.	✔	✔	
Grandma thinks it's cute when it farts.	✔		
It can actually fetch big stuff you throw.			✔

other. The dog dropped the ball at Barry's feet and looked up, staring Barry square in the eye.

One poodle joke and you die, said the dog. It so happened that Barry didn't know any poodle jokes, although he always kind of wondered how poodles survived millions of years of evolution when meanwhile the saber-toothed tiger goes extinct.

Maybe cavemen thought poodles were cute

and knitted little jackets out of goat wool or dried seaweed to protect them. You never know.

***

Before you interrupt: yes, I know I just made a poodle talk. But it wasn't right out loud, okay? In this story I'm pretending that animals can communicate like mind readers. As if they have telepathy.* And who's to say it isn't true: I mean, you never see them put up satellite dishes or paint billboards just to send messages to each other.

> Q. Hey, no fair! How come the fleas get to talk right out loud?
> A. That's different.

***

The dog must have figured Barry was okay, because now he relaxed and introduced himself: *I'm Vladimir Guerrero. Throw the ball anywhere and I'll fetch it.*

***te-*LEP*-a-thee** Telepathy is the ability to communicate without talking or writing or wiggling your eyebrows. Some people say they are telepathic when they really aren't. But there's just no talking to them.

Barry snickered. Vladimir Guerrero looked hurt, so Barry explained that Vladimir Guerrero the human was one of the great baseball players of today, that he played for the Expos and the Angels, that he roamed the outfield with the grace and speed of a gazelle, that he could hit almost any pitch. Then Vladimir Guerrero the dog said, *They named a baseball player after me? Cool. What's baseball?*

Barry just shook his head, picked up the tennis ball, and bounced it in one hand. He looked out across the lake, then back at Vladimir Guerrero, grinning.

Race ya, Barry said—Barry telepathied—and he whipped the ball as far as he could. Before it even hit, Barry and Vladimir Guerrero plunged into the lake after the ball, splashing frantically out into the murky, fish-stinky water. It looked exactly the opposite of a boy and his dog trying to escape from a shark.

I'm With Stupid looked up and slowly stood.

Vladimir Guerrero easily reached the ball first and was already paddling back with it before Barry was even halfway there. Barry quickly changed directions and flailed back toward shore, but Vladimir Guerrero easily passed him on the way back too.

Barry was exhausted by the time he finally dragged himself on shore, shaking, coughing, and gasping for air. Vladimir Guerrero stood calmly in his glossy wet coat with the ball in his mouth and his head cocked to one side, looking a bit disappointed.

I'm With Stupid helped Barry up. "Kid, you okay?" he said. Then he got a funny grin on his face and he wiggled a finger toward Barry. "Hey!"

Barry looked down.

His pants were gone.

Somehow, somewhere out there in the big lake, Barry's big baggy werewolf-disguise pants had come clean off, right over his

VLADIMIR GUERRERO

Height: 6' 3" Weight: 225 Bats: Right Throws: Right
Born: February 9, 1976, Nizao Bani, D.R.

2004 Stats

G	156	HR	39
AB	612	RBI	126
R	124	AVG	.337
H	206	OBP	.391
2B	39	SLG	.598
3B	2	OPS	.989

***VLAD*-ih-meer ger-*RARE*-oh** Vladimir Guerrero is one of the great baseball players of today. He roams the outfield with the grace and speed of a gazelle, and he can hit almost any pitch. He once hit a homer off a pitch that bounced in front of the plate first.

shoes, without him noticing, and now he was standing there with water dribbling like rain from a leaky drainpipe down the front of his Jockey shorts, his Y-fronts, his tighty whities.

Shivering.

***

I should have mentioned this before: it was not exactly the warmest day of the year.

***

Maybe in a week or so Barry's pants will be discovered washed up on rocks and kept as possible evidence in a murder case.

***

Barry stomped away as fast as he could in those squelchy shoes and that heavy, sopping sweatshirt, with cold peanut butter soup starting to ooze through the stitching in the bottom of his knapsack.

He could hear I'm With Stupid behind him just laugh and laugh.

The great wall of flowers

I don't know about your town, but where Barry lives there is no particular law against boys walking around outside in public in their underpants, wet *or* dry. Not that I've exactly looked it up, though.

But it is certainly *frowned upon*. "Frowned upon" is when somebody doesn't like what you're doing but can't think of anything specifically *wrong* with it.

Barry had been walking, being frowned upon, for quite some time now, more or less back in the general direction of his house, mostly because he had no good reason to go in the general direction of anywhere else.

He came to a nice red fire hydrant just as he needed to pee, probably from accidentally gulping so much awful lake water. No wonder fire hydrants are popular with dogs: they're so *convenient*.

Although Barry was already 96.9 percent boyhound on the inside, he still had just enough boy brain to remember to check around for spies. A look of deep concern came across his face and he glanced left and right; then he casually propped one foot up on the hydrant as if he were going to tie the laces of his shoe. Gazing up, he saw some words painted high on the side of a large brick building, appearing against the sky like holy graffiti:

DON'T MAKE ME COME DOWN THERE.

—God

***

Being 97.2 percent boyhound now, Barry had no clue what the words said, if anything. He just scowled up at the letters and let a little yellow trickle travel down his leg, flow around his ankle, and dribble into the other shoe. Then he turned like nothing had happened—as if he hadn't just peed himself, as if now one shoe wasn't even squelchier than the other—and he continued innocently walking.

Except *walking* is not entirely the right word to describe a boy, who is actually a dog, slumping along in wet underpants, schlepping a soggy knapsack, and wearing a dripping sweatshirt with a peanut butter stain spreading across the back, who is shivering and in a hurry to get somewhere—anywhere—so long as it's warm.

I know: how about *you* think of a verb? Why do *I* have to do everything?

***

I'm waiting . . .

Got one? Good. Let's try it out:

So there was Barry, [verb]-ing down the sidewalk, when all of a sudden he saw one of those glassed-in bus stops, so he [verb]-ed right over to it and quickly [verb]-ed inside.

***

Barry crouched in a corner of the bus stop. It was empty and smelled of fumes and coffee and chop suey and sweat. *That's nice,* thought Barry.

Just as he was getting cozy, Barry saw it: a squashed frog was plopped right there on the sidewalk, its arms and legs splayed wide open and in perfect symmetry, as if it were pinned down for a biology experiment or posing for an ink-blot test.

Except this frog had been trampled by hundreds of impatient bus riders, or possibly smoked by the bus itself, and now it was flat and dusty and leathery brown and stiff, like a

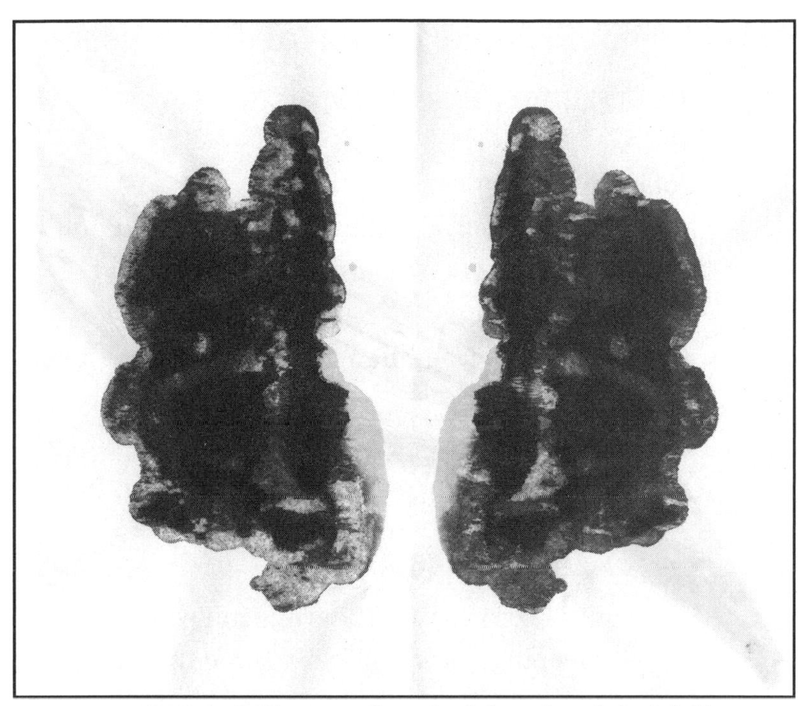

HER-man RORE-shok Hermann Rorschach introduced the ink-blot psychology test. You look at pictures of ink blots and say what they remind you of, and your answers are supposed to reveal how your brain works. For example, if you say "a squashed frog," they'll probably let you go home. But if you say "a helicopter wedding cake," they'll probably call your parents. When in doubt, always say "a squashed frog."

miniature catcher's mitt somebody forgot in the garage all winter.

Barry bent forward and nudged the frog with his nose. It scooted easily across the ground, smooth as cold toast on linoleum. This was a lot of fun for Barry, and he quickly thought up a whole bunch of fabulous new boyhound games, for example:

Follow the Frog:
: Push the frog around with your nose until you just get tired of it.

Capture the Frog:
: Flick the frog, then go chase it before it gets away.

Find the Frog:
: Pretend the frog is hiding from you, then find it under your foot.

Wake the Frog:
: Bark and bark at the frog, and when it keeps sleeping, bark and bark some more.

You're probably right: boyhounds aren't too good at coming up with cool stuff to do with a stiff frog.

Up there on Barry's head

Flea Two screamed blue murder. Flea One had grabbed the base of the hair and was shaking it as hard as he could. Flea Two clung on for dear life to the top of that very hair while Flea One shook it back and forth and back and forth and back and forth and back and forth.

FLEA TWO: Stop!
FLEA ONE: No!

FLEA TWO: Stop!
FLEA ONE: No!

They shouted at each other. Sheesh. It was awful.

But hey, at least they were *talking,* which I guess is maybe a tiny bit better than saying nothing at all.

Meanwhile

One by one, a few people meandered into the bus stop, but Barry didn't seem to notice. He was down on his hands and knees, busily playing Sniff the Frog: get real close and sniff the frog a million times in case the smell changes for any particular reason.

Barry got a little tired of this game after a while, plus the rough sidewalk was making his bare knees and elbows sore. He slowly got up on his knees, only to come face to face with a massive wall of flowers that spread as far as the eye could see.

Barry leaned in and nuzzled his nose into the soft middle of the big pillowy wall, wiggled it into a good warm spot, and took a great big deep breath.

Except these flowers didn't smell anything like flowers.

To say the least.

Just as he was thinking, *Huh, these flowers smell exactly like some lady's giant behind,* something smacked him in the side of the head, and a loud voice from above shrieked, "You disgusting boy, how dare you!"

The lady spun around, and her massive flowery dress flapped like a flag on a frigate* and whumped Barry hard right across the face.

As Barry tried to stand, she clobbered him in the chest with something hard and lumpy in a plastic shopping bag—a pot roast or half a dozen turnips—knocking Barry out of the bus stop and sending him skidding onto the sidewalk.

Just then the bus came, and everyone stampeded Barry as he lay there on his

*__*FRIH-get*__ A frigate is a fast warship. You put a flag on your frigate so everybody knows whether to wave hello or sink you with torpedoes.

stomach, stunned. Along the way somebody jabbed him in the ribs with a pointy shoe and called him "an animal."

Sometimes people can be so entirely right for entirely the wrong reasons.

Then the bus pulled away and finally there was quiet.

***

One minute later, Barry crooked his aching head to one side with the effort of rolling a boulder from the mouth of a cave. Lying next to him on the sidewalk was the frog, probably booted there in the rush and now even flatter than before.

Barry groaned and stood up. He was about to turn and walk away, but the frog's dead, dusty eyes seemed to follow him.

Barry looked down at the lonesome frog.

He tried to look away.

But his heart softened.

He looked back again at the frog.

He gave a little sigh.

Oh, all right, c'mon, little buddy, Barry thought to the frog. He stooped and, with his lips wrapped over his teeth, Barry lifted the frog by a leg, gently clenching it, and wandered off with the little leathery mitt bouncing against his chin.

***

Finally one hundred percent pure boy-hound, Barry sensed a low rumbling—an approaching thunderstorm, or hunger, or possibly both.

Peanut butter sandwiches

As before, Barry had been walking and walking. Except now he was even more scraped up and more sore and more achy all over and more tired.

But let's look on the bright side: at least now he was a lot less wet and a little less cold.

Plus, he was now pretty close to his school, and pretty close to home, if you think that belongs on the bright side of things.

The frog had been dangling from Barry's mouth the whole way, slapping and slapping against his chin, and they had been frowned upon and frowned upon for a good couple of miles now.

Barry never did notice the frowning, though; animals just don't *get* frowning. It's only humans who have difficulty accepting things as they are.

Suddenly Barry heard a familiar clanging sound and immediately his mouth began to water. It was the lunchtime bell at his school, but all Barry's boyhound mind knew—or cared about—was that the sound of that bell was always quickly followed by something nice to eat.*

Barry remembered his two plain peanut butter sandwiches.

He snuck around to a back corner of the schoolyard and found a patch of bare earth behind a tree. He carefully nestled the frog on

***ee-*VAN PAV*-lov** Ivan Pavlov was a scientist who experimented with dogs in order to understand humans. He found that when he rang a bell, then fed a dog, soon enough the dog would also get hungry when just hearing the bell. Maybe he forgot that most dogs are hungry all the time anyhow.

George Washington Carver was an important agriculturalist who discovered hundreds of new uses for soybeans, sweet potatoes, and peanuts. His work boosted the economy of the American South and nutrition for everybody. He didn't invent peanut butter, though. Strawberry jam neither. Or toast.

a fresh bed of maple leaves, then grunted and wrestled and groaned to get his knapsack off. It took forever.

***

You probably know this already: whenever you wrestle a knapsack, the knapsack usually wins.

***

Barry unzipped the knapsack and tossed out a couple of mushy, pulpy notebooks smeared with runny ink. He reached in again and felt around for the sandwiches,* which had long ago been squished through their wrapping and now formed a mucky layer of sludge at the bottom.

Barry thought for a moment, then slipped the knapsack over his head like a hangman's hood or a lame last-minute Halloween costume, and sat there in total darkness, gnawing hungrily upward at the goo.

*See APPENDIX II if you want to try my peanut butter sandwich recipes.

Soon enough Barry heard the scurrying of lots of little feet along the branch above him, and then a sound halfway between chickens clucking and the loud kissy noises your friends make when they suspect you have a girlfriend.

Squirrels.

Barry stopped gnawing for a second to listen.

He heard a telepathic voice: *Hey, pooch! Yeah, you, betcha can't catch us, poochie, poochie, poochie.*

Normally, a boyhound doesn't wait around for a special invitation to go chase squirrels. But Barry was tired and sore and hungry and had a knapsack over his head and was in no mood right now.

Whaddya mean, you're in no mood? telepathied the voice. And then, *Pee-yoo, you smell funny. What kinda dog are you anyhow?*

Barry was about to answer when he realized he did not in fact know what kind of dog he was, what kind of dog he had turned into overnight like magic.

You don't know? Sheesh. This made all the other squirrels laugh and cluck even louder. *Anyhow, I'm Monica. This is my tree. Whatcha eatin'? Mmmm, smells peanutty. I love peanuts. Whatcha got? Can I have some? Roasted peanuts? Peanut brittle? Peanuts in the shell? Chocolate-covered peanuts? Peanut surprise? Peanut soup? Peanut salad? Peanuts with the skins on? Peanut satay? Peanut delight? Peanut-crunch topping? Peanut crumble? Peanut log? Peanut loaf?*

And so on and so forth ad nauseam.*

***

In case you never noticed: squirrels can't relax. They're permanently nibbling, con-

***ad NOZ-zee-um** "Ad nauseam" is a polite Latin way to say that somebody has been talking so much it makes you just want to throw up.

stantly fussing and fidgeting. They always have somewhere to go in some big fat squirrelly hurry, change their minds halfway there, and go in some big fat squirrelly hurry in the opposite direction. Must be something in the nuts.

***

Barry lifted off the knapsack and squinted into the sudden daylight to see probably twenty squirrels in a row, hovering like a gang of wingless vultures along a branch, which swayed under their weight.

Their beady black rodent eyes were fixed on Barry, who had peanut butter streaked through his hair, dabbed on his nose, and smeared around his mouth, plus clods of wet peanutty bread wedged behind his ears and rolling down his sweatshirt, which you may remember had a peanut butter stain in the middle of the back.

Peanut butter! Why didn't I think of that! Monica said by telepathy. *Crunchy or smooth?*

That question made the others fidget even more excitedly than before and they elbowed each other out of the way for a closer look.

Barry realized he was pretty much surrounded and sensed trouble.

Dogs, boyhounds, and other animals tend to be right when it comes to this stuff. They can smell it.

Monica telepathically shouted, *Get him, girls!*

Barry froze to the spot—mostly because he had nowhere to run even if he could, and also because he couldn't believe he was about

Whenever you close this book, the hyena gets the gnu . . .

to be mugged by a bunch of furry nut-nibblers one-billionth his size.

And then of course that's exactly what happened.

All at once twenty squirrels leaped off the branch and pounced on Barry like a pack of hyenas on a wounded gnu, like black ants on a red lollipop, like distant relatives at a wedding buffet.

They quickly swarmed over Barry, knocking him flat, licking and tickling his face, biting and hurting his nose, pulling at his hair, and sneaking off to hide tiny wads of peanut buttery bread like they were nuggets of gold,

. . . and whenever you open to this page, the gnu escapes.

then scampering back to gather more. Barry rolled himself into a ball, closed his eyes tightly, and covered his face. Some squirrels jumped on his back, scratching and gnashing the sweatshirt where the peanut butter had seeped through; others wriggled under the sweatshirt, digging their claws into Barry's skin, to eat from the inside out, leaving a nearly perfectly round eight-inch hole, as if Barry himself had cut it out with scissors, as if it were in fashion.

Monica clucked an order, and just as suddenly the squirrels all vanished, none wanting to be marooned on that delicious but funny-smelling dog that didn't even know what kind of dog it was.

***

It seemed safe now. At least it was quiet.

Barry carefully opened one eye, then the other, in time to see one final, fat squirrel disappear around a far hedge, dragging the knapsack behind her, clumsy as a monkey stealing a lawn mower.

With a groan Barry sat up, encircled by tufts of shredded sweatshirt fluttering over the ground as if they were trying to erase the scrabbling of claws. He reached to touch his nose and winced at the sting; hundreds of tiny cuts and scratches covered his body, mostly on his face and back, and each one delivered a tiny sharp sting of its own.

Barry blinked the dirt out of his eyes and looked around. Suddenly he gasped. He crawled over to see.

His heart sank.

It was the frog.

Poor little innocent dead frog. It had been torn apart in the attack. Only one hind leg remained attached to its body, so now it was deader than ever.

Barry knelt to dig a hole for his friend, though the earth beneath the tree was hard and dry and thick with roots. But he did his best, and by the time he'd dug deep enough, his hands ached and he bled under the fingernails. With his scratched, stinging nose Barry nudged the frog into the shallow grave, then let the dusty earth sift through his fingers until it was covered.

"Barry!" said a sudden voice. Barry jumped up. The Brothers were standing there. "Everybody's been looking for you."

"Yeah," said the other Brother, biting an apple.

Barry spun around.

The Brothers ran screaming.

FAIR WARNING

YOU NEVER KNOW WHAT'S GOING TO HAPPEN WHEN YOU SNEAK UP ON A BOYHOUND

Stanley Cup parade

Ask yourself which is more frightening:

A. A scary monster hiding in your closet
B. A scary person hiding in your closet

Practically everybody, when they think about it, picks B.

Maybe that's because we know there is no such thing as monsters, so we don't know what we're supposed to be afraid of exactly; monsters are too *abstract*.*

***AB-strakt** Abstract things have no real shape and can't be described, like a kaleidoscope design or the art of Jackson Pollock. Pollock was famous for dribbling paint all over his canvases, and that's not scary at all unless you happened to have been his cleaning lady.

But we do know what people are capable of, so it's easy to imagine horrible things. That's why the Brothers ran screaming: they figured Barry was still a boy, still their friend, who just decided to go totally psycho for no good reason.

One millisecond after Barry jumped up in surprise and spun around, the Brothers jumped back in horror, suddenly seeing all his cuts and bruises, the dirt and torn-out hair, his air-conditioned sweatshirt and tighty-whitey underpants, which were neither tight nor white anymore, and his bleeding fingernails and everything.

Barry was scary.

More frightening, Barry had a fierce, rabid look in his eyes as he hunched his shoulders, held the Brothers in a wild fiery stare, and snarled viciously.

Grrrrrrrrrrrrrrrrr, snarled Barry. It wasn't especially loud, but it came from deep within his throat, what they call "guttural." It was real.

This surprised Barry more than anyone. His new boyhound brain hadn't realized how much anger and hurt and confusion had been boiling up inside, ready to explode at the slightest thing. Which just so happened to be his two best friends and an apple.

So the Brothers ran screaming, arms waving wildly, back toward the school as the bell rang to end lunchtime.

If you were minding your own beeswax, looking out a classroom window at this particular moment, you might think that the Brothers were good students rushing back to class so they would not miss a single minute. Except then you'd also see Barry tackle the slower Brother by the leg and yank him to the ground with an ugly thud.

***

In case you are taking notes: the faster Brother just kept on running.

***

Like an octopus glommed on to a deep-sea diver's helmet, Barry wrapped himself around the Brother's leg and bit his ankle again and again, making him cry as much in pain as in disbelief.

The Brother kicked and kicked at Barry with his other foot, blindly, desperately, and finally kicked himself free and staggered through the school doors, disappointing the small crowd of students who had gathered in hope of a better fight.

But he did not escape before sacrificing a trophy to Barry's triumph: one sneaker had slid off in the scuffle, and Barry seized the sweaty prize and thrust it proudly overhead for all to admire, as if it were the Stanley Cup or the head of Saint John the Baptist.

At that exact moment, storm clouds con-

Saint John the Baptist was a great prophet during the time of Jesus, and was in fact Jesus' cousin. But John was so popular that it angered the jealous wife of the Roman ruler Herod Antipas. She demanded that John's head be chopped off and delivered to her on a platter. Which only made John more popular than ever.

nected overhead like heavy black pieces of a giant jigsaw puzzle and everything went dark. A bolt of lightning sliced through the air, and with a crack of thunder the rain came down like a guillotine. Barry arched his back to catch the rain in his mouth and then, doused in victory, he spat it back out and shook his head and howled up at the applauding sky.

Up there on Barry's head

Flea One stopped shaking the hair and stopped shouting. He stepped back, folded his arms, and squinted up through the torrential rain at Flea Two.

FLEA ONE: *Don't tell me—you jumped up there to see if you'd turn into a mosquito overnight like magic and fly away happily ever after. Am I right or am I right?*
FLEA TWO: *No.*
FLEA ONE:
FLEA TWO: *I didn't jump. I shinnied.*
FLEA ONE: *Whatever. And now you can't get down.*
FLEA TWO:
FLEA ONE: *Just slide down. It's nice and wet now.*
FLEA TWO:
FLEA ONE: *Or you could always jump. You're a flea. A flea can jump higher than a kangaroo!*
FLEA TWO:
FLEA ONE: *What? What? Did you say something?*
FLEA TWO: *I said I'm scared of heights.*

Meanwhile

Barry felt glorious and reborn, as if all the microscopic cogs and wheels in his brain had ground to a halt, then rapidly started turning in the opposite direction, somehow realizing they'd made a terrible mistake.

That's the thing with boyhounds: they forget the past almost as fast as it happens. And the future is only the present that they haven't gotten around to yet.

A BOYHOUND BUMPER STICKER

TODAY IS THE FIRST DAY OF THE REST OF TODAY

Like magic the downpour stopped and the clouds rushed off somewhere else to spoil a picnic or soak bedsheets on a clothesline. Even though the storm left Barry completely drenched for the second time that day, it also recharged his energy and he now felt as light as a champion.

Barry trotted smack down the middle of a quiet street lined with quiet houses and quiet old trees whose leaves sprinkled droplets of water like fat confetti onto Barry's victory parade. Stupidly happy with the rubbery

Stanley Cup bobbing in his jaws and dripping filthy slobber, Barry was also stupidly lucky that there weren't too many cars at this time of day.

As he pranced along, Barry already could not entirely remember how he won this tasty trophy. Oh well. It didn't really matter.

He came to a house that looked kind of familiar.

It was Barry's house. You probably guessed.

He couldn't wait to go inside and show his mom the sneaker. *She'll be so proud,* thought Barry.

Just to let you know: Barry's boyhound brain did not allow him to think the actual words "She'll be so proud." It was really only the wobbly idea that if he brought the sneaker into that house, the person inside would surely be most pleased to receive it.

Barry scooted around to the back door. (Hardly anybody used the front unless they were maybe trick-or-treating or delivering Chinese food.) He crouched and silently inched the door open to await the perfect moment.

His mom was sitting with her elbows on the kitchen table and her face buried in her hands. Her shoulders were quivering. To any normal boy she might well have been giggling and playing peekaboo with the coffee cup.

But being a boyhound, Barry could immediately tell that his mom was extremely unstupidly unhappy, although he couldn't imagine any reason why she should be so sad.

This will cheer her up, thought Barry, and he clenched the sneaker more tightly in his teeth.

To Barry the moment was now; to a boyhound it always is.

ANOTHER BOYHOUND BUMPER STICKER

THE MOMENT IS ALWAYS NOW

He banged the back door open, leaped into the middle of the kitchen floor in a single bound, flung his arms out wide, gave a huge grin, and shouted:

"Ta-da!"

Except it actually came out as:

Arr-RAAAAAH!

And the sneaker dropped from his mouth, hitting the floor with the moist thud of a bowling ball landing on a bed of petunias.

Mrs. Barry's Mom jerked her head up at the sudden noise. Tears were streaming down her cheeks.

Almost an entire second of completely empty silence ticked by.

Mrs. Barry's Mom just stared, astonished, shocked, horrified. Her jaw, as they say, hit the floor.

Barry just stood there grinning his silly grin. Still grinning, he twitched one eyebrow, then the other, and held a tiny shrug.

WHAAAT?

And then:

"Barry! There you are! The school called! Nobody knew where you were! I've been worried sick! Barry, look at you! What happened? Are you okay? Answer me, Barry! Barry! All right, have it your way, young man! You're in big trouble now! Oh, Barry! Those cuts and bruises! Your clothes! My poor baby! Let me look at you! I'm so glad you're all right, Barry!"

Mrs. Barry's Mom went through the entire *5 Phases of Upset Mothers* in only one small paragraph, setting a new personal record.

***

They ought to put her picture in *The Guinness Book of World Records.*

***

Somewhere between Phases 4 and 5, Mrs. Barry's Mom moved across the room and

The 5 Phases of Upset Mothers

When you do stuff that really worries your mom, she goes through these five phases, in this exact order. Phases may blend together and last for different amounts of time—especially Phase 3, which can go forever, depending on what you did.

1. **RELIEF, PART I**
   The brief initial phase when your mom is just happy that you didn't run off with the circus and get a tattoo.

2. **CONCERN, PART I**
   Just because you didn't do anything drastic and permanent, you are still subject to strict interrogation, which may result in close medical supervision and/or disciplinary measures.

3. **ANGER**
   Now your mother thinks you're a schnook. Typically the longest phase, Anger may last one minute to several hours, even weeks. Strive to vacate the building during Anger.

4. **CONCERN, PART II**
   Oh, great, now you made her feel guilty, you schnook.

5. **RELIEF, PART II**
   But that's okay. At least you didn't run off with the circus and get a tattoo.

held Barry tightly in her arms, but not too tightly in case it hurt him.

The thing with boyhounds is that they don't know very many actual words; words are just details and not very important ones either. So this is pretty much all Barry's boyhound ears heard:

"Barry! Yadda yadda yadda! Yadda! Barry, yadda! Yadda? Yadda? Yadda, Barry! Barry! Yadda yadda big trouble! Oh, Barry! Yadda!"

Yet somehow Barry understood perfectly. A lot of times you don't need to understand somebody's words to understand what they're saying.

Unfortunately, opposites also have a habit of being true. For example, when you say nothing at all, you will always be misunderstood. Which, any old boyhound can tell you, only leads to more trouble.

As Barry was about to find out.

98.6°

Mrs. Barry's Mom led Barry by the wrists and sat him down on a kitchen chair. Expertly, wordlessly, she examined every inch of Barry like a triage* nurse on a battlefield or someone choosing a cantaloupe.

She sifted her fingers through Barry's dirty, matted, tugged, and torn-out hair.

She gently touched his scratched-up nose, ears, and back, his bruised arms and legs, and his bloody fingernails.

**TREE-ahj* Triage is when there are so many injured people that a nurse has to decide who gets treated first. If you're only scratched, forget about it. If you're dead, forget about it. If you're somewhere in between, take a number and please be seated.

She noticed the pants that weren't there.

And everything.

Mrs. Barry's Mom stood up, went to the sink, and came back with a large bowl of lukewarm water, a washcloth, and a crinkled tube of antiseptic cream.

She stripped Barry down to his not-so-tighty-not-so-whities and dabbed him all over with the wet cloth.

Mrs. Barry's Mom was cycling through the *5 Phases* all over again, and decided to linger on Phase 3 for a while. The dabbing got just a little rougher.

"You've really done it this time, Barry. What have you got to say for yourself? Hmm?"

Barry, of course, didn't have anything to say for himself. He didn't have anything to bark or yelp or arf for himself either. He just held his tongue, confused that bringing home the Stanley Cup didn't go over as nicely as he'd planned. And he held his breath with the pain of merciless dabbing.

"Nothing. Just as I thought," she said, now smearing the cream all over Barry. "When your father comes home, we are all going to have a very serious talk."

***

Mrs. Barry's Mom brought some clean clothes for Barry. She also brought a thermometer and took his temperature. It said 98.6 degrees Fahrenheit.*

"At least you don't have a temperature," she said.

***

Before you interrupt: yes, of *course* Barry has a temperature. I *know* that. It is 98.6 degrees Fahrenheit. What Mrs. Barry's Mom meant to say is that Barry did not have a *high*

*__FARE-un-hite__ Named after German scientist Daniel Fahrenheit, who made thermometers long ago. You can also measure hot and cold on the centigrade scale, which is based on the freezing and boiling points of water. They use different numbers just to confuse you.

temperature, that he did not have a *fever,* that he is not going to have to lie in bed *sweating* to death and then *shivering* to death and then falling asleep and having scary dreams about ugly polka-dot monsters in cowboy boots playing the *accordion.*

a-*KORD*-ee-un Just squeeze 'n' play.

A useful reminder: no matter how bad things may seem, accordion music can always make it worse.

***

As you probably know, 98.6 degrees Fahrenheit is normal body temperature—for humans, anyway. (Just for the record, an actual furry, four-legged dog is usually around 101.5 degrees on the inside.)

As you also know, body temperature is pretty much the only normal human thing about Barry on this particular day.

***

Then Mrs. Barry's Mom said the best thing in the entire world if you happened to be a 98.6 degree human boy. She said, "You'd better stay home from school the rest of the day."

Well, okay, maybe it wasn't the *best* best thing in the entire world. I mean, it's not like she said:

> Here are some free wrestling tickets, *or*
> There's only birthday cake for dinner, *or*
> You can wear those underpants all week.

But still.

Then she said something maybe not so great: "Barry, go lie down in bed."

That's right. Mrs. Barry's Mom had shifted into Phase 4. At least she didn't make him swallow any medicine, which is usually the bad part about staying home from school. Just a glass of water and no pills.

Of course, Barry did not understand a word his mom said. But she was shooing him up the stairs, so Barry obeyed.

Barry found a room that smelled familiar, but he didn't get into the bed. The mess of old laundry on the floor looked much comfier. He circled three times around the small oval rug, curled up in the middle of it, and nuzzled his face into a stinky damp pile of yesterday's socks and undies, exhausted.

***

Yes, I know it sounds dumb, but it actually is okay to say that you can "circle" around something that is "oval." But do me a favor: try not to say it very often in case I'm wrong about that.

On the other hand, you definitely cannot "oval" around something that is a "circle." I mean, please, I do know *that* much about geometry.

***

So Barry was lying there on the floor, snuggled up on the rug at the foot of his bed, drifting off into gentle doggie dreamland, as quiet as a buried bone, as silent as an old slipper, as whispery as a warm cat on a windowsill. Soon enough, he was swirled up in a dream about sinking in a huge bowl of quicksand

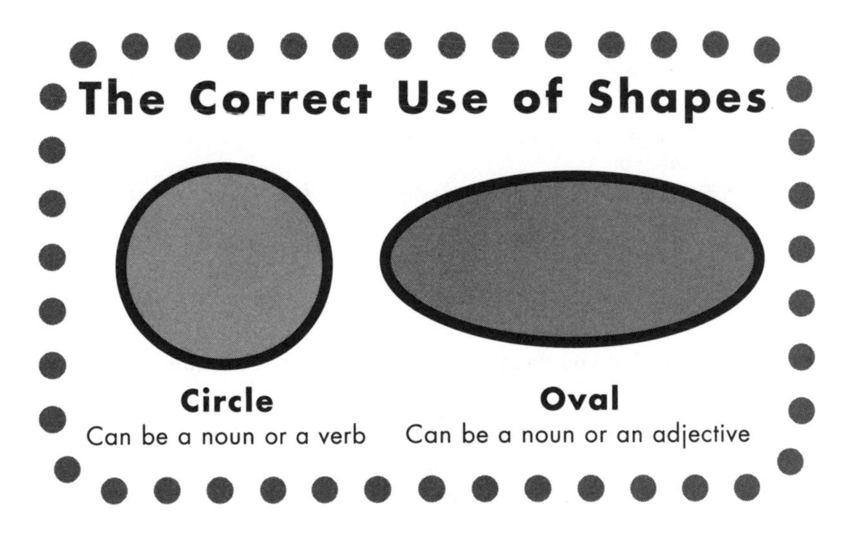

popcorn shaped like tiny raccoons . . . and his leg twitched.*

Up there on top of Barry's head, however, there was quite the arthropodal† ruckus going on.

Up there on Barry's head

Suddenly Flea One stopped shaking the hair and shouting. He stood back, folded his arms, and squinted up at Flea Two.

> FLEA ONE: *Well, that's just dandy. If you're scared of heights, it's a good thing you didn't turn into a mosquito overnight like magic.*
> FLEA TWO: *Oh? Why's that?*
> FLEA ONE: *Who ever heard of a mosquito that's scared of heights? Mosquitoes fly around all the time. You'd be scared your short little entire life.*
> FLEA TWO: *Hmm . . . yeah, maybe.*
> FLEA ONE: *But you're not scared of being a flea, are you?*
> FLEA TWO: *Of course not.*
> FLEA ONE: *Then you're lucky. If you were a mosquito, you'd spend the whole time wishing you were a flea.*
> FLEA TWO: *I see what you mean.*
> FLEA ONE:
> FLEA TWO:
> FLEA ONE: *Shinny back down, buddy, and let's go scare up some scalp. I'm starving.*

* See APPENDIX III if you feel like reading a sample boyhound dream.

†***AR*-thro-pod** Arthropods are what scientists call insects, spiders, and crustaceans. Fleas are only one kind of arthropod. There are millions more. In fact, there are more arthropods crawling around than all other kinds of animals put together. It's creepy.

Meanwhile

Barry was woken by a sudden itching on his head.

He scratched.

He yawned.

He ached.

He licked himself too, but that antiseptic cream tasted just awful.

He stood up and stretched, and all the little cuts and stings sprang back to life. Then his stomach growled so loudly Barry was sure that there must have been another dog in the room—and he actually growled back.

Barry had woken up hungry, as all boys, dogs, and boyhounds do. Please remember, all he's had so far today is milk, cereal, peanut butter goo, and a worm, and although that already covers several important food groups, he was still not fully satisfied.

He craved moist, congealed meat and meat by-products, beef tallow, corn gluten meal,

EVER WONDER WHAT MAKES YOUR STOMACH GROWL?

Pardon my language, but that growling in your stomach is caused by gas that's moving and squelching around in there.

It gets even more disgusting if you want to keep reading.

Okay, you asked for it.

When your brain decides it's time to be hungry, and you haven't eaten anything yet, the walls of your stomach squeeze together to mix up the gases and digestive juices.

Doctors and scientists call this growling "borborygmi," which is a nifty Greek word they use so they can discuss noisy stomachs around the dinner table without anyone knowing what they're talking about.

beet pulp, glucosamine, sodium bentonite, biotin, lecithin, and calcium propionate to preserve freshness.

You guessed it: Barry wanted plain old dog food.

He crept downstairs and into the kitchen.

Aha! There it was, over there, next to the garbage can: a bowl—with a whole pile of food in it.

Barry scampered over for a good whiff.

Eww! Barry jerked his head back. *Smells . . . fishy!*

> Oily silver skin—*yup*.
> Scratchy little bones—*yup*.
> Eyes—*yup*.
> Mashed up with a fork—*yup*.
> Real stinky—*yup*.

Yup, it sure was fish in that bowl. Sardines, if you must know.

Okay, so it wasn't quite what he had hoped for, but it did almost count as food. Barry figured, quite correctly, that when you are positive there is nothing else, it is actually possible to eat fish.

Besides, like all dogs, boyhounds think it's best to eat first and ask questions later.

WHAT A DOG BELIEVES:
"Hey, You Can Always Barf Later"

This is not dog food. Barry's wobbly, foggy doggy mind was puzzled. *This is more like food for a—*

—then he spun around and saw it.

Pitter-pattering across the linoleum floor behind him.

The purring gave it away.

Barry had entirely forgotten—

—his family had a

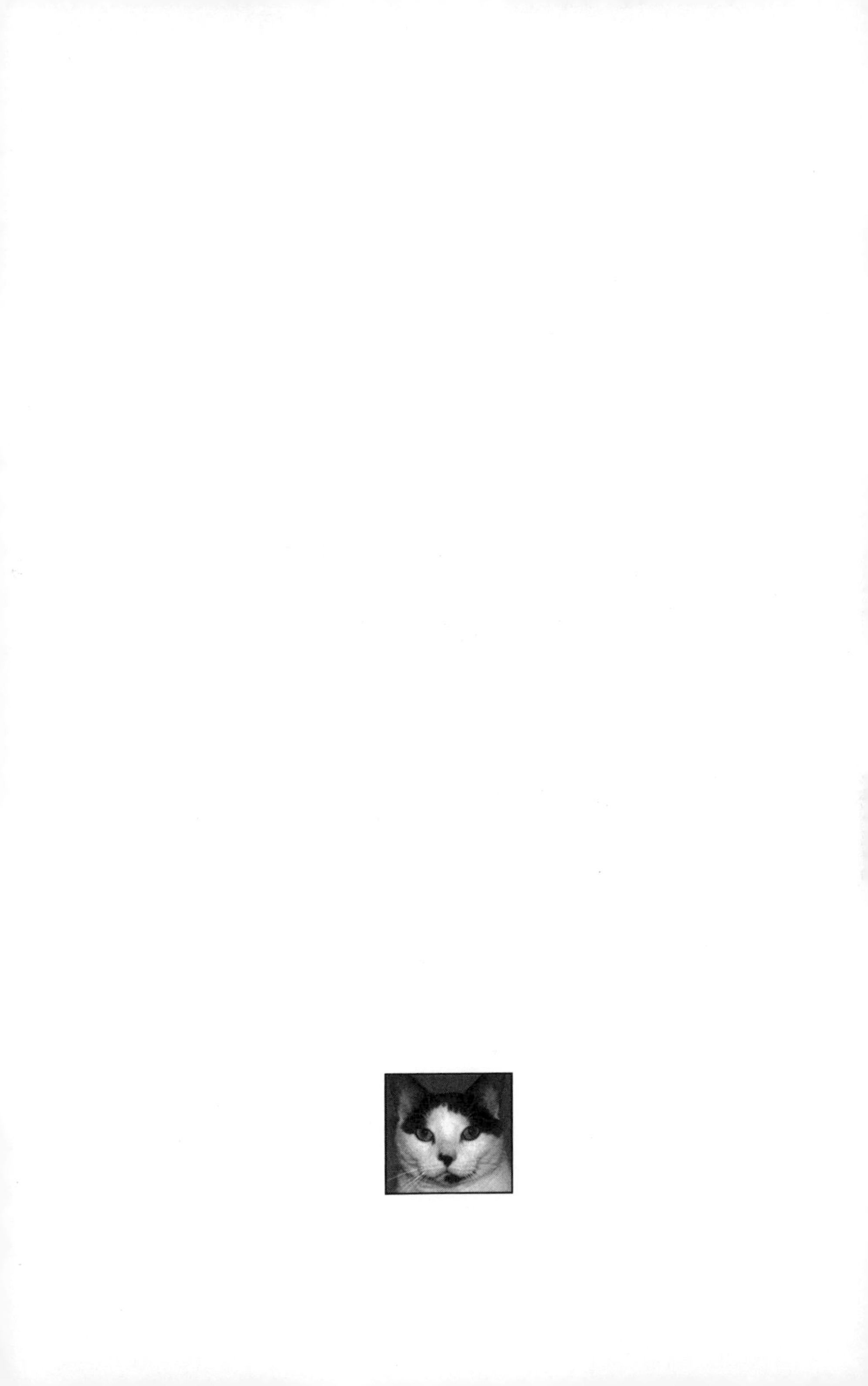

12

Kerrrack!

Barry looked at the cat.

The cat looked at Barry.

Barry and the cat looked at each other for a hundred years, which was actually only half a second or maybe less. In that half a second or maybe less, the cat knew something was entirely different about Barry. That's because animals have this thing called "instinct."*

Instinct is when you know something but

***wane *GRET*-ski** Wayne Gretzky was the best hockey player ever. They say he had "instincts" because he always knew where the puck was going. But it's not the same kind of instinct. He was great because he was really smart and he practiced a lot.

don't know you know it. All animals have instinct, and they don't even have to stay up late to study for it.

***

Humans don't need much instinct; instead we have big huge brains to help us think, learn, and remember. I don't mean "learn" in the way you learn to not wipe yourself with poison ivy, or that the square of the hypotenuse of a right-angled triangle is equal to the sum of the squares of the other two sides.

I mean the way you learn how to be a person and decide what's important to you. Mushy stuff like that.

***

The cat knew this was not the same Barry who tickled her under the chin and is supposed to clean out her litter box with a spatula every morning like he always promises his mom he will.

"I promise," Barry always said before they got the cat.

"I forgot," Barry always said after they got the cat.

***

Cats don't argue with instinct. They don't hang around and discuss it during their lunch break either:

> CAT: Barry doesn't seem his usual self—pass the fish, please.
> INSTINCT: That's curious. Perhaps he turned into a boyhound overnight like magic or something.
> CAT: Should I amscray? Hightail it out of here? Mmm, these scratchy little bones are *divine*.
> INSTINCT: Suit yourself—coffee?

No. The cat's instinct had exactly one thing to say about it: *Run!* the cat's instinct yelled at the cat.

So the cat ran as only a cat can run.

The very millisecond the cat's instinct figured out that Barry was a boyhound, this is what happened:

1. First, her fluffy white fur stood right up on end.
2. Then she arched her back and made one of those really horrible cat noises that no one can spell.
3. Then she spun around the kitchen floor trying to get a good grip with her claws.
4. Then she ran very, very quickly straight up to Mrs. Barry's Mom's room and hid under the bed among the shoe boxes. And she didn't bump into a single thing the whole way.

Up there on Barry's head

Boy, were Flea One and Flea Two ever full. Neither of them could suck another drop. They drank so much of Barry's blood, all they could do was lounge around on springy bits of dandruff, having a burping contest.

FLEA ONE: *RRRRRAAAALLFFFFFFFF!!!*
FLEA TWO: *No fair! That was fake!*
FLEA ONE: *Okay, you win.*
FLEA TWO: *Listen, I just want to say sorry for that.*
FLEA ONE: *No, you were right. It* was *a fake burp.*
FLEA TWO: *No, I mean, sorry about before—all that I-want-to-be-a-mosquito stuff.*
FLEA ONE: *Oh. That. Never mind.*
FLEA TWO: *You must think I'm a real schnook.*
FLEA ONE: *You're not a schnook to want something from life. You'd be a schnook* not *to.*
FLEA TWO: *Yeah? You really think so?*
FLEA ONE: *Sure.*
FLEA TWO: *So what is it that* you *want from life?*
FLEA ONE:
FLEA TWO: *What's wrong?*
FLEA ONE: *Oh, nothing.*
FLEA TWO: *You're blushing.*

Meanwhile

By the time Barry reacted to all this, the cat was already upstairs and under the bed with her heart pounding in terror. Barry's reaction was as slow as a dentist's office, as slow as a new bottle of ketchup, as slow as a strawberry Pop-Tart in an unplugged toaster.

Barry just stood there for a second. If Barry had had any boy brain left inside, it probably would have told him to just leave the cat alone, for crying out loud.

But no. Barry's dog instinct told him to go chase the cat because, well, that's what dogs do. So Barry ran as only a boyhound can run.

You may wonder: how the heck does a boyhound run, then?

Answer: nothing like a cat.

***

Just to let you know: one of the most important boyhound skills is to become a silent hunter of cats and/or squeaky toys. Although Barry was still a clumsy beginner, he was in fact quite silent. He got that much right.

Oh, he was the Silent Primeval* Predator all right, creeping silently across the carpet on his belly, nostrils flared to detect even the faintest feline scent, his squinty predator eyes fixed on the silent cluster of shoe boxes under the bed, where the cat would surely be hiding, quivering in fear, hopelessly awaiting her horrible fate at the merciless hand of Barry, boyhound, Silent Primeval Predator.

***

Barry already had quite an array of impressive boy skills. For example, he could perform a perfect oreobotomy† by neatly twisting open

***pry-*MEE*-vul** This is a way of saying that something is as ageless and unchanged as the gases that make up the rings of Saturn. The hunting behavior of predators has existed for millions of years—longer than *Tyrannosaurus rex* or the rules of chess.

†*OR*-ee-oh-*BOT*-to-mee The surgically precise removal of an Oreo cream center.

an Oreo and gently teasing the cream up with his tongue without leaving a single white smudge on the cookie part.

The list goes on, but since the cat is still "quivering in fear" and so on, it would be cruel to make her suffer a moment longer. So let us now return to "the merciless hand of Barry" and his prey.

***

Barry steadied himself, poised to pounce. He bared his teeth and drew a deep breath, but instead of pouncing he accidentally inhaled an entire dust bunny—and he sneezed. It was very loud, you should have heard it (the sneeze, not the dust bunny).

Once again the cat bolted like lightning:

Kerrack!

She scattered the shoe boxes as she ran. One of the lids flew off and hit Barry neatly between the eyes like a tomahawk, leaving a perfect pink dent there.

Ow! thought Barry.

***

You'd be amazed how much an innocent piece of cardboard hurts when it hits you exactly right.

***

Barry got up, a little stunned. He turned to run after the cat, but his foot got tangled in the cord of his mom's bedside lamp. He

EER-o-kwoy The Iroquois are a nation of native North American tribes including the Cherokee, Mohawk, and Seneca. Europeans called them "Indians" even though they were at least ten thousand miles from India. The Iroquois used tomahawks to hunt animals and defend themselves against people who were looking for Calcutta.

toppled face-first, and the lamp slid off the night table and hit him smack in the back of the head as he fell, knocking him out cold.

He didn't even have time to think *Ow!* this time.

He was silent.

The cat, as you probably guessed, could be just about anywhere by now, and probably was.

Mrs. Barry's Mom, as you probably also guessed, could be in only one place by now after all that racket.

"Barry!" Mrs. Barry's Mom shouted, straddling the sprawled Barry with her hands on her hips. "Barry! *What* in the name of *Pete* do you *think* you are *doing*? *Answer* me!"

And being knocked out cold was going to be no excuse.

13

x = feeling like a schnook

Mrs. Barry's Mom bent down and shook Barry by the shoulder. His head swarmed with angry bees; his tongue was coated in prickly unflavored carpet fuzz.

"Barry, get up." She was none too pleased with her murdered lamp and the cord strangling Barry's ankle. She was none too pleased with her slippers and sandals and high heels strewn randomly across the floor as if they'd begun to escape, then just got tired of the whole idea. She was none too pleased with Barry.

She was about to explode when she felt the large swelling on the back of his head—Barry's big shining lamp lump—and her voice softened. "Oh, Barry," and she just shook her head.

Barry was still groggy a minute later down in the kitchen, holding a woolly sock stuffed with ice cubes against his lump. The sock smelled clean. *You can't have everything,* thought Barry.

WHAT CAUSES LUMPS?

Lumps can be caused by a variety of things, depending on where you find the lump:

On Your Head

caused by fluids in your body collecting at the affected area to provide cushioning and to heal an injury

In Your Throat

caused by fear or peanut butter

In Mashed Potatoes

caused by insufficient mashing

Silently Mrs. Barry's Mom waited for an explanation of what in the name of Pete Barry thought he was doing—or for the swelling to go down enough so that she could get mad at him again, whichever came first. That's the thing with some people's moms: the less they say, the more they make you feel like a schnook.

You know, we could be in for a long, boring wait, waiting for Mrs. Barry's Mom waiting for Barry. If this were a TV show, this is when they'd play a bunch of commercials for microwaveable oatmeal with cinnamon 'n' raisins and toys that provide hours of fun until they break in twelve minutes.

But this isn't TV. All I can show you is what a couple of teensy little fleas have been up to lately.

Up there on Barry's head

If you remember, Flea Two realized it was silly to want to be a mosquito, to want to be anything it was impossible to be. He also realized that it's important to have a dream, to want to be something he *could* be. So he asked Flea One what *his* dream was, and that one simple little question made Flea One blush like crazy.

Blushing is when you get all embarrassed and your face goes all hot and red. I'm sure you already know fleas can't actually blush. As Mark Twain said, "Man is the only animal that blushes—or needs to."

FLEA TWO: *C'mon, c'mon, tell me, why are you blushing?*
FLEA ONE: *No. It's embarrassing.*
FLEA TWO: *Pleeeeeez?*
FLEA ONE: *Well . . . okay—promise not to tell?*
FLEA TWO: *Tell who?*
FLEA ONE: *That's a point. Okay. My dream is to join the circus.*

One of the greatest writers in the English language, Mark Twain wrote the classic books *Tom Sawyer* and *The Adventures of Huckleberry Finn*. His real name was Samuel Langhorne Clemens.

FLEA TWO: *The circus. Uh-huh.*

FLEA ONE: *I want to walk the tightrope! Swing on the flying trapeze! Jump through burning hoops—*

FLEA TWO: *Burning hoops?*

FLEA ONE: *Of FIRE!! Of course, at first I'd be willing to do a clown act or whatever, to learn the ropes. . . .*

FLEA TWO: *I see.*

FLEA ONE: *But soon they'll call me "the Great Flealini"—*

FLEA TWO: *The Great what?*

FLEA ONE: *And they'll come from miles around to love me! To adore me! To worship at my feet!*

FLEA TWO: *Excuse me, but loving you and worshiping at your feet are not the same thing.*

FLEA ONE: *Huh? How do you mean?*

FLEA TWO: *Well, for example, I love you—as a friend—but I'm not gonna worship at your feet, okay? Besides, you have far too many feet to worship at.*

FLEA ONE: *Really? I mean, you really love me?*

FLEA TWO: *Well, as a friend, yes, absolutely—I mean, let's not get carried away.*

FLEA ONE: *Does this mean I don't have to jump through burning hoops—*

FLEA TWO: *Of fire? No. Totally unnecessary.*

FLEA ONE: *What a relief! Thank you.*

FLEA TWO: *No prob.*

FLEA ONE: *Can you still call me the Great Flealini anyway? TGF for short? Whatever's more convenient.*

Meanwhile

Barry has still not come up with a good explanation for the lamp and the lump and the shoes scattered like narcoleptic* jailbreakers, never mind the cuts and scratches and sweat-shirt and pants. And he never will.

NAR-ko-lep-see Narcolepsy is sometimes known as "the sleeping disease." It's not really a disease, though. It's actually a condition in which narcoleptic people suddenly fall asleep at odd times and in strange places. Other people just go to the opera.

What to Be or Not to Be

Words and music by Andy Spearman

No, you cannot be what you cannot be
May as well wish that you were taller than a tree
Think of all the great things a person might be
Any one of which presents a possibility

You can save all the whales, eat all your peas
Win a million dollars in a lottery
Fix your granny's bathtub, then take her out to sea
Find a cure for loneliness or solve a mystery

You can go to California with a banjo on your knee
Or load up the truck and move to Beverly
Build a log cabin on the shores of Zuider Zee
Or cut off your hair, sit down and watch some TV

[chorus]
Now you can be anything that you can be
So if you were a flea, then you'd have to be a flea
Now this is just a guess, but you're a human like me
So you can be whatever you decide to be

Even if Barry could speak, he couldn't remember. A boyhound's memory is as short as a sneeze, short as a sunny Saturday, short as a ride on a roller coaster.

Let me put it this way:

$$x \leq [(a - b) \div \Delta c] \bullet \pi r^2$$

where

x = feeling like a schnook
a = remembering stuff for like more than two seconds
b = 11.3
Δc = turning into a boyhound overnight like magic
πr^2 = running around in circles for no good reason

As promised, Mrs. Barry's Mom got mad.

She demanded to know what had gotten into Barry, she wondered how she could have such an evil child, she pointed out that the Brothers seemed like nice boys and asked why Barry couldn't be more like them, she asked if Barry knew the price of replacing the lamp and the sweatshirt and the pants, she asked whether Barry could conceivably imagine what would happen once she discussed this with his father.

And what did Barry hear the whole time? That's right: Yadda yadda, Barry, yadda.

He did know one thing for sure, though. She seemed to think he had done something bad. What, he had no clue. Except that it made her feel bad. Which made Barry feel bad.

As Mrs. Barry's Mom spoke, Barry slid off his kitchen chair and crawled around to where she sat. Kneeling there, he rested his chin on her lap, looked up at her with big goofy eyes, and pouted.

Suddenly Mrs. Barry's Mom didn't know what to do. She stopped talking, then she did what everybody does when a sad woofy dog wants a hug: she played her fingers through his hair and lightly tugged his ears.

A moment passed between them. For Barry it was a moment of simple affection; for Mrs. Barry's Mom it was utter confusion, and she wondered what kind of doctor she might have to call.

Mrs. Barry's Mom didn't know what to say. All she could think of was "Janey will be home from school soon."

Whatever, thought the boyhound, who didn't understand a word his mom said. *Whatever makes you happy.*

***

What Barry no longer remembers is that he and Janey seldom make each other happy; until today, they were pretty much normal brother and sister.

But Janey remembers. You see, Janey keeps a diary,* and it's full of big fat secrets about her mean brother, Barry. As I'm sure you know, a diary is a book that nobody is allowed to read.

Forever and ever.

And ever.

Ever.

***

I know what you're thinking: how come I

*See APPENDIX IV if you want to read a page from Janey's diary.

know what's in Janey's diary if nobody is allowed to read it?

Answer: I was very naughty. I peeked.

***

They weren't always that way, though. Barry thought Janey was an okay sister at first—when she was a baby and slept all day—but then she learned to walk and talk and then everything changed and she became so annoying.

Soon enough Barry felt as if *all* Janey *ever* did was squeal on him all the time:

> Mom! Barry put Ken in the microwave!
> Mom! Barry peed on the toilet seat again!
> Mom! Barry said to get out of his face!
> Mom! Barry hid gerbil poo in my pillowcase!

You get the picture.

But very soon, something truly awful is going to happen to Barry, and Janey won't even have to squeal on him this time. Everybody is going to find out all about it anyway.

Everybody.

— ONE FREE SPANK —
• for diary peeking •
This coupon entitles the holder to give exactly ONE spank to
ANDY SPEARMAN
Photocopy this page. Cut photocopied coupon along dotted line. Save. One spank per customer. No fair collecting a whole bunch of coupons to get extra spanks.

SPEARMAN SPANK SPECIAL
TERMS AND CONDITIONS
BY ACCEPTING THIS COUPON YOU AGREE TO THE TERMS AND CONDITIONS HEREIN. THIS IS A LIMITED-TIME OFFER, WHICH IN FACT EXPIRES 30 DAYS AFTER PURCHASE OF THIS BOOK, SO IT'S PROBABLY TOO LATE ALREADY. REDEMPTION OF COUPON IS SOLELY THE RESPONSIBILITY OF THE SPANKER. IN OTHER WORDS, IF THE SPANKEE IS NOT AVAILABLE FOR ANY REASON WHATSOEVER, THAT'S JUST TOUGH LUCK. I MEAN SERIOUSLY, WHAT WERE YOU EXPECTING? VALUE OF COUPON DOUBLES IN THE EVENT THAT YOU PERMIT SPANKEE TO PEEK AT YOUR DIARY TOO. YOUR CONSTITUTIONAL RIGHTS ARE NOT AFFECTED BY THIS OFFER. NO CORRESPONDENCE WILL BE ENTERED INTO. VALID ONLY IN TAHITI. COUPON HAS NO CASH VALUE. EVEN LESS IN CANADA.

14

Some big fat disaster

Slam! went the back door.

"I'm home!" Janey shouted. She didn't actually need to shout. Her mother was sitting right there at the kitchen table, with Barry curled around a chair leg at her feet.

Janey plunked her knapsack down and skipped over to where Barry happened to be gently licking the open palm of his very confused mother. Janey stopped dead when she saw this, her mouth dropped open, and she instantly became Barry's very confused sister.

***

What on earth am I going to do? Mrs. Barry's Mom had been wondering for some time now.

Mmm, salty, was all Barry had been thinking.

***

Janey tiptoed backward and scowled at the two of them. Then she said what she always says whenever she accidentally sees somebody's pink slobbery tongue in action:

"Ewww!" said Janey. And then again: *"Ewww!"*

Mrs. Barry's Mom quickly wiped her hand on her knee and cleared her throat; Barry slouched over to the other chair and sat and stared at the tabletop.

Janey decided to ignore what she had just seen; after all, she had exciting news to report.

"Barry got in a fight at school today. I bet he never told you that, didja, Barry, huh."

Janey looked at the cuts and scrapes on Barry's face and rolled her eyes. Mrs. Barry's Mom looked sternly at Barry.

"Never mind," said Mrs. Barry's Mom, but Janey told her anyway about the Brother and the ankle and the sneaker. Most of it was pretty much true, but Mrs. Barry's Mom still couldn't quite believe it, even if it did explain the sneaker. She kept staring a hole through Barry.

"Never mind," said Mrs. Barry's Mom.

"There was blood everywhere and stuff like that," which of course wasn't true at all. And finally, "I can't wait till Dad comes home tomorrow, oh yeah."

On any other day—and there were thousands to choose from—just thinking about a mad Dad, just thinking about the 7 Dadly Sins, would give Barry major heebie-jeebies. But not today. Not on boyhound day. Today: nothing, nada, diddly-squat.

The 7 Dadly Sins

Dads usually get mad in a different way from moms. But sooner or later they figure, Hey, it's not like you spray-painted the car orange or anything. That's why the 7 Dadly Sins are really six sins plus one way dads might try to make it up to you, though don't hold your breath.

1. Wrath	Go to your room right this second!
2. Ire	You want to be grounded forever? You got it, mister! Forever! And I mean it this time!
3. Anger	I've had quite enough of your tomfoolery and shenanigans, thank you very much!
4. Vexation	Where do you think you're going! Come back here right this second and clean up the big mess you made and/or flush the toilet and/or say sorry to your sister and/or your mother!
5. Consternation	What are you standing here for? I thought I told you to go to your room! Now go back there right this second! Forever!
6. Disappointment	I just don't understand why you have to be such a schnook! Now, when I was your age . . .
7. Atonement	Hey, c'mon downstairs. Wanna play catch or something, bud? Go get an ice cream?

"Whatcha got there?" said Mrs. Barry's Mom, leaning around to see what Janey had been hiding behind her back, trying hard to sound cheerful, trying hard just to change the subject.

It worked. All at once Janey's eyes sparkled. She jiggled with joie de vivre* and with a big round smile she revealed something from behind her back with the flourish of a magician making a real live African elephant appear before your very eyes.

"A marionette!" Janey proudly held up her latest school Art project. "His name's Pierre and I can make him dance, lookit." Janey tap-danced Pierre back and forth across the kitchen table, and Barry watched out of the corners of droopy, resentful eyes.

jwah de *VEEVE *Joie de vivre* means "the joy of life." When the French have better words to describe happy things, the English steal them, which makes the French a bit unhappy. Then they say *C'est la vie* (**say la *VEE***: "that's life" or, in other words, "tough petunias").

Ever since turning into a boyhound, Barry has not given much of a hoot about Art. Animals simply don't care what something *represents* or what it *means*. To an animal Art is just short for Arthur.

"Why, that's just lovely, Janey," said Mrs. Barry's Mom, who always gives a hoot about Art. She wasn't picky, though. For her you didn't need to be a genius like Leonardo da Vinci or Jimi Hendrix.

To the boyhound, however, Pierre simply looked like this:

1. Kraft Macaroni and Cheese box: one head
2. Googly eyes: two
3. Magic Marker mustache: one
4. Toilet paper tubes: two arms; two legs; one neck
5. Paper towel tube: one abdominal region
6. Crepe paper: shirt, tie, vest, and trousers
7. Pipe cleaners: too many to count
8. Not-quite-dry-yet glue: gobs and gobs
9. Long red woolly string: a whole bunch

"Can I go play outside with Pierre till sup-

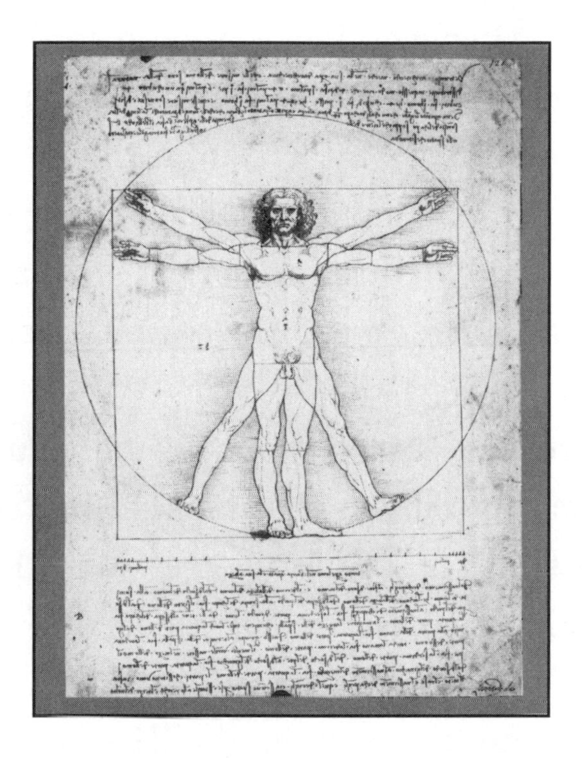

lee-oh-*NAR*-doe dah *VIN*-chee Leonardo da Vinci was one of the most important people of the Italian Renaissance. He was most famous for painting the *Mona Lisa,* but da Vinci was also a great scientist. He designed irrigation systems, drew detailed studies of human anatomy, and had the first idea for a helicopter five hundred years ago. But Jimi Hendrix could wipe the floor with him on guitar any day.

per's ready?" That's the thing with sisters: oh, sure, it's okay if *they* go and totally wreck their own Art project in two seconds, but if a *brother* wrecks it even one tiny bit, then, oh, now suddenly it's some big fat *disaster*.

Also: whenever Janey wanted to play outside, which was every single day except when there was maybe a tornado in the backyard, Mrs. Barry's Mom always made Barry go too, and Barry hated being forced to play with Janey, because *c'mon,* she's a *sister,* and she throws like a *girl*.

"Sure, go ahead, Janey." And you don't need me to tell you that for the first time in the History of the Universe, Mrs. Barry's Mom didn't ask Barry to go too.

But this time Barry didn't wait to be asked—another first in the History of the Universe—because the moment Janey opened the back door, Barry saw his precious trophy sneaker lying on a back step, where Mrs. Barry's Mom had probably chucked it in case it spewed germs or started to attract weasels.

In a sudden burst of energy, Barry jumped up, swooped past Janey, scooped up the

tor-*NAY*-doe A tornado is an extremely strong whirlwind that spins at 300 miles per hour. The funnel-shaped cloud forms when a huge mass of cold, dry air bumps into a huge mass of warm, moist air, and it destroys everything in its path. So if you lived near here, it wouldn't be a very good idea to go outside and play right now.

sneaker, tucked it under one arm like a football, and ran around the backyard in sloppy figure eights as if someone kept switching the darned goalposts.

Janey stood in the doorway holding the

marionette by the strings, laughing so hard at her dumb brother that she bounced Pierre up and down until it seemed he was laughing at Barry too.

***

A useful reminder: one of the worst things that can happen in this life is to be laughed at by a puppet.

***

Mrs. Barry's Mom came up behind Janey and spoke into her ear. "Barry's not himself today." Even though Mrs. Barry's Mom had no idea who (or what) Barry was today, she was certainly going to try very hard to find out.

That's the thing with moms: somehow, sooner or later, whether you like it or not, they wind up knowing *everything*. Moms even beat Santa Claus in this particular regard.

Janey just shrugged. She didn't think

Barry was himself today either. No, Barry was entirely different. Today, Barry looked like fun. So Janey skipped out to the yard, dragging Pierre along by his long red woolly string hair.

SANTA CLAUS vs. MOM

SANTA	MOM
Gives presents	Gives presents
Gone by morning	Makes breakfast
Big white beard	Usually no beard
Fits down chimney	Fits through door
Lives at North Pole	Never been there
Knows when you are sleeping	Knows when you are sleeping
Knows when you're awake	Knows when you're awake
Knows when you've been bad or good	Knows when you've been bad or good
Knows quite a lot	Knows *everything*

Up there on Barry's head

Now it was Flea One's turn to wander off alone somewhere on Barry's scalp and slump down heavily on a heap of old dandruff scraps, sad as a worn-out tire in a rainy junkyard. But Flea Two had been following quietly behind; he knew from experience that Flea One could maybe use a friend right about now.

FLEA TWO: *Why the long face?*
FLEA ONE: *Very funny.*
FLEA TWO: *Look, I wasn't saying that joining the circus was a dumb idea.*
FLEA ONE: *Yes, you were.*
FLEA TWO: *I was saying, fine, if that's your dream, then you have to stop dreaming about it.*
FLEA ONE: *Stop dreaming about my dream?*
FLEA TWO: *Exactly.*
FLEA ONE: *Well, that's just brilliant, Mister I Want to Be a Mosquito.*
FLEA TWO: *I've been doing some thinking since then.*

But Flea One had stopped listening long before, so Flea Two figured he might as well stop talking.

Meanwhile

Not wanting to muck up her fluffy yellow slippers in the damp grass, Mrs. Barry's Mom stood in the doorway, hollering at Barry to come back inside, but he just didn't seem to hear. Janey ignored her too, and she danced Pierre in the middle of the lawn, spinning in circles as Barry ran big goofy loops around them. Janey giggled and staggered with dizziness, and Barry yelped in delight.

Mrs. Barry's Mom stopped hollering for a second and raised her hands to her lips as if she had suddenly decided to pray. If you couldn't see inside her brain to know what she was thinking, you might guess that she was praying for maybe a swimming pool to magically appear, or at least for someone to please come and mow the lawn.

She was in fact having a far stranger thought. For the first time ever in the History of the Universe, she saw that Barry and Janey were not fighting, were not arguing. Just the opposite: they were actually having fun together. That's right: they were *frolicking*.

***

Just to let you know: weirder things have happened, though I can't think of any examples right now.

***

However, Mrs. Barry's Mom's nice warm frolicky thought lasted maybe three seconds.

Because then:

All of a sudden Barry flung the sneaker aside and pushed Janey to the ground, and Pierre went tumbling as Barry pinned her down and licked her face, and Janey laughed and shrieked and half pretended it was totally gross. Then Barry turned rough, and Janey's laughs quickly turned to cries of pain. Startled, Mrs. Barry's Mom hopped down the steps in her fluffy yellow slippers and flip-flopped into the yard like an angry duck as fast as anybody wearing fluffy yellow slippers possibly can.

And then:

Barry rolled off Janey, clamped his teeth around Pierre's toilet paper tube neck, and shook him and shook him, harder and harder. His snarling and growling scared Janey even more.

And then:

Barry jumped up to escape the angry duck and ran behind the crab apple tree, clenching the marionette in his droolly jaws. His saliva made Pierre's toilet paper tube neck all soggy and soft. In the next second Pierre's body ripped completely in two—his bottom half flew off and landed on a branch of the crab apple tree, and the long red woolly string, attached to Pierre's head and limbs with gobs and gobs of not-quite-dry-yet glue, got all stuck and tangled up in Barry's hair.

And then:

In a panic Barry ran down the driveway, waving his arms wildly, with the long red woolly string streaming behind his head.

If you were far enough away—for example, if you were minding your own beeswax sitting on a porch across the street and you just so happened to look up in time—it would've looked almost exactly like Barry's head was on fire.

Janey and the angry duck both ran down the driveway after him, yelling and yelling.

But Barry was way faster. And without looking, without listening, without thinking, he ran straight out into the road.

The History of the Universe

If you had to whittle it down to only three people, you could say the History of the Universe was written by Isaac Newton, Albert Einstein, and Stephen Hawking. The universe is 15 billion years old, but our understanding of it is very new, and we certainly don't know it all. Three hundred years ago, Newton figured out the Laws of Gravitation and Motion. This explains why lasagna hits the floor when it slides off your plate but also how planets orbit around the sun and how our whole galaxy works. In the twentieth century, Einstein came up with the Theory of General Relativity, which shows that outer space doesn't just go on forever in a straight line. No, time and space warp each other so that the universe has a kind of oval, or elliptical, shape. Hawking said that the universe is always getting bigger, so obviously it must have been much smaller before. But that doesn't mean the universe just began on a Tuesday when there was nothing else to do. Then it gets tricky because Hawking says that there must be an end to the universe, but also that there are no boundaries—like the inside of an expanding balloon. Nobody knows for sure how, where, or why the universe began—and a lot of intelligent people disagree. Human science can't explain everything because the facts of science keep changing. But when we learn one thing, it lets us learn another, so our facts keep getting better. After all, only 550 years ago it was a "fact" that the world was flat. A useful reminder: facts are only the current opinions of experts.

15

Something Truly Awful

Ever notice how in action movies whenever a car goes driving off a cliff or an army guy jumps from an exploding jeep or a bridge collapses in an earthquake, they always, always, always show it in slow motion?

Slo-mo. It's what they call a Hollywood cliché.* Here's why they do it every time:

1. Well, it looks really cool.
2. That's how it seems in real life when Something Truly Awful happens.

*__klee-*SHAY*__ A cliché is the same old way of doing something, when it's old hat, worn thin, warmed over, dull as dishwater, like a broken record, old as the hills, and bores you to tears till the cows come home.

People report that when Something Truly Awful is happening to them in real life, everything seems entirely different. Everything gets louder to their ears. Everything gets sharper to their eyes. Everything gets stronger to their nose. Most of all, everything gets much, much slower to their mind.

HOL-lee-wood This is a place in California where most of the movies in the United States are filmed. When they first put this sign up in 1923, it read "Hollywoodland." It's shorter now but it's just as tall: each letter is 50 feet high.

I'm sure there is a perfectly good explanation for this phenomenon,* and I would make no bones about telling you if I happened to know what it was.

***

Just to let you know: I don't know everything.

Up there on Barry's head

Flea Two had stopped talking and began pacing back and forth across Barry's scalp, thinking very hard, making Barry quite tickly up there. So Flea One began talking, as those who have stopped listening tend to do. He said that being a circus flea was a noble profession for insects of their stature *and for another thing* it sure beat hanging around sucking the blood of some stupid *dog* with such a *schnook* for a friend.

Flea Two didn't hear a word; he was too busy thinking of how he might explain himself.

Finally:

> FLEA TWO: *The way I see it, having a dream is great—every flea needs one—but there comes a point—*
> FLEA ONE: *Let me guess—a point when you have to* stop dreaming, *right?*
> FLEA TWO: *And work toward the dream—exactly!*

***fuh-NOM-uh-non** A phenomenon is a strange fact or event you might not be able to explain using normal logic. It can even stump intelligent scientists. More than one phenomenon are called *phenomena,* which can really get scientists confused—it's *phenomenal.*

FLEA ONE: *Huh . . . ? Work . . . ? Toward . . . ?*
FLEA TWO: *Yeah. Otherwise that's not having a dream. It's just dreaming.*
FLEA ONE: *There's a difference?*
FLEA TWO: *All the difference in the world.*

Meanwhile

Barry ran in a blind panic with long red flames of woolly string flowing from his head. He ran down the driveway and into the street, without looking, without thinking, without stopping, as crazy as if his head really were on fire.

So he never even saw the car coming.

But Janey and Mrs. Barry's Mom did see the car, driving maybe a little too fast, and then everything became slow and loud and sharp and strong—especially their scream:

"Barry!

Watch

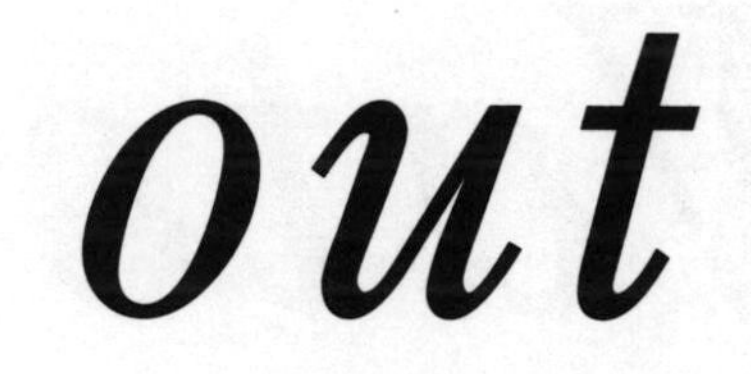
out

for

the . . .”

. . . Too late.

16

A bunch of baloney

Up there on Barry's head

Flea One was so mad at Flea Two.

So mad.

He was mad because, hey, he goes and saves his friend's *life* and what thanks does he get? *Insults* about joining the noble circus! A bunch of *baloney,* a load of *malarkey,* a barrel of *squit* about having a *dream*! Shoulda left him twisting slowly in the *breeze* on the top of that stupid dog's *hair! Humph!**

***

Flea Two felt so bad about Flea One.

So bad.

He felt bad because, hey, his friend saved his *life* and

*__HUMF__ To say this word, close your mouth and quickly force air out through your nose. But please practice carefully or you'll blow snot all over your shirt.

what did he do in *return*? He made him feel bad about having a dream entirely by *accident*.

I know what you're thinking: maybe Flea Two shouldn't've said anything at all, because sometimes that's the best thing to do when friends get mad.

But the way Flea Two looked at it, when something's really important, you have to say it even if it is hard to say, even if you wind up making your best friend feel bad entirely by accident.

***

A useful reminder: the most important things are always the hardest things to say. Always.

***

As much as Flea Two had already said, there was still more he felt he needed to say. The thing is, Flea One wasn't sure if he needed to listen.

FLEA TWO: *Listen, I'm sorry—*
FLEA ONE:
FLEA TWO: *What I said before, well, maybe it came out all wrong—*
FLEA ONE:
FLEA TWO: *I mean, I still meant it—*
FLEA ONE:
FLEA TWO: *You know, about dreams, dreaming and all that—*
FLEA ONE:
FLEA TWO: *But—*
FLEA ONE:
FLEA TWO: *I didn't mean it the way I said it—*
FLEA ONE:
FLEA TWO: *I mean, I didn't mean to make you mad—*
FLEA ONE:
FLEA TWO: *I was just trying—*
FLEA ONE:
FLEA TWO: *To help a little—*

FLEA ONE:
FLEA TWO: *Because dreams are so important and—*
FLEA ONE:
FLEA TWO: *Well—*
FLEA ONE:
FLEA TWO: *Um—*
FLEA ONE:
FLEA TWO: *Can I tell you something?—*
FLEA ONE:
FLEA TWO: *It's more of a question, really—*
FLEA ONE:
FLEA TWO: *Is it okay if I come with you to the circus?*

Meanwhile

The screaming siren was the first thing the entire neighborhood heard; then they all came out and saw the flashing lights, and finally, screeching to a halt at the foot of Barry's driveway, the ambulance itself.

17

Mushy old papaya

If only Barry could see himself right now, lying in the hospital bed, swaddled in bandages from head to toe, entirely like an ancient Egyptian mummy.

That's one difference between us and the ancient Egyptians: they bandaged people up into mummies after they were dead; these days we bandage people up like mummies to try to stop them from getting dead in the first place.

Not that it would be fair to let Barry die from running out in front of the car, from being hit by the car.

TOOT-un-*KAH*-mun Tutankhamen (King Tut) is famous because no one discovered the treasures in his tomb for 3,000 years. Otherwise he was not very important. Just another rich Egyptian teenage king.

Not at all. If you read to the end of this story, you will see that it is not as sad as all that. This is more of a happy story. Just to spill the beans.

***

A useful reminder: in real life, not counting umpires, there is generally no one standing there to decide what's fair or not.

***

Beneath the wrapping, Barry had a quadrillion cuts and scrapes over every inch of his body—you'd think he'd been practicing kung fu* inside a cement mixer driving down a bumpy road.

His leg was broken too, and now it was coated in a hard plaster cast rigged up to a rope and pulley that hoisted his leg above the bed—a drawbridge raised over a river flowing with wavy white hospital sheets. Just to try another metaphor.

*There are many martial arts in the world, and Bruce Lee was the greatest expert in jeet kune do. Nobody *ever* beat him in the movies or in real life, except once, when he was a teenager, but never mind about that.

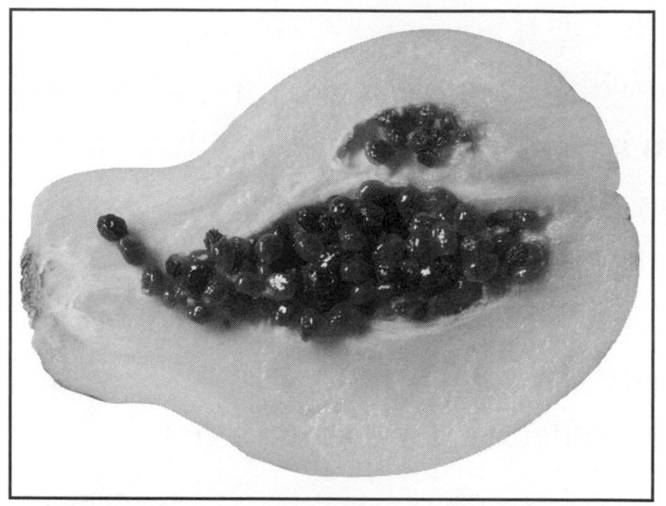

puh-*PIE*-yah They call the papaya a wonder fruit because it's full of vitamins A and C, potassium, and beta-carotene. It also helps you digest other foods that taste good but maybe aren't quite so wonderful for you.

Worst of all, Barry had a big huge bump on his forehead that had now swollen to a size far larger than the one from his mom's flying lamp. This new lump was the size and smudged orangy yellowy color of a mushy old papaya.

I know what you're thinking: that must hurt like all get-out.

And believe you me, as soon as Barry regains consciousness, as soon as Barry *comes to,* he'll be the first to agree with you.

***

Mrs. Barry's Mom stood next to the bed, softly gazing at lumpy, scratchy, plastered, swaddled Barry. With one finger she slowly twirled a tuft of his hair that poked through a gap in the bandages at the top of his head.

Janey stood nervously next to her. She was nervous because it was weird being inside an actual real hospital for once—a hospital that wasn't on TV—where the air was filled with odd smells and boredom and pain. She was nervous because maybe this was all somehow her fault—well, at least her fault *and* Pierre's. Mostly she was nervous because, as Truly Awful as it looked, she didn't know that Barry was not going to die.

***

Let me know if you think it's cruel, but I haven't gotten around to telling her that yet.

***

By the way, Barry, since the accident, has

not moved one inch, one smidgen, one iota,* one jot, one hair, one micromillimeter, one teensy-weensy little bit.

Barry was knocked out cold, colder than freezing pee in a snowsuit when it's minus eight billion degrees out, as Barry can certainly tell you.†

Too bad, because Barry has missed all the action even though he was smack in the middle of it—it was *ironic.* At least a dozen dramatic, scary, noisy things have happened since the last time Barry can remember anything:

1. He got hit by a car that tried to stop but couldn't.
2. It wasn't the driver's fault; he's usually a good driver.
3. Barry slumped to the ground.
4. Janey screamed and screamed.
5. Mrs. Barry's Mom screamed a bit too.
6. The ambulance came with its siren screaming.

***eye-OH-ta** *Iota* is a letter of the Greek alphabet, and for some reason it also means "a tiny bit." The Greek letters *delta, pi,* and *omega* also have extra meanings. In fact, *alphabet* comes from the Greek letters *alpha* and *beta*. So much of English isn't very English.

†See APPENDIX V for the story of when Barry peed in his snowsuit.

7. They lifted Barry onto a stretcher.
8. Janey screamed and screamed some more.
9. The ambulance drove away with its siren screaming.
10. They arrived at the hospital and carried Barry in.
11. They rushed him into the emergency room.
12. They did tests and X-rays, treated his cuts and scrapes, set his broken leg, bandaged his lumpy head, and so on, and now he's lying in bed with a mummy body and a drawbridge leg and he won't remember a single thing.

For the record: every once in a while somebody out there gets a bump on the head and entirely forgets who they are, whether they like asparagus, and what the capital of France is. They get *amnesia*. And then, every once in a much, much longer while, that same person goes and gets another bump and everything comes back to them in a flash, like this: *Norbert, yucky, Paris*. The other 99.9 times out of a hundred, including Barry, boyhound or not, a bump on the head is just a bump on the head, and it hurts like all get-out.

Up there on Barry's head

Flea One stared in absolute amazement at Flea Two; he just stood there with all six hands on his hips, nodding his head slowly and a little suspiciously.

You just be quiet: I *know* that technically fleas don't have hands or hips. And while we're at it, wisenheimer, I very much double dog doubt that any actual real flea could "stare in absolute amazement" either. Actual real fleas do not stand around trying to figure stuff out; their instinct tells them they have far better things to do.

Mind if we get back to the story now? Thank you. Any more questions? Good, then. Any more extremely rude interruptions? Thank you. Need to go to the bathroom or anything? Hunky-dory. Sheesh.

The thing is, Flea One wasn't sure if he was supposed to be happy about what he thought Flea Two had said, or if maybe he ought to get mad all over again. Flea Two was getting him all mixed up and stuff.

FLEA ONE: *So . . . you mean—*
FLEA TWO: *Yes.*
FLEA ONE: *But I thought you said—*
FLEA TWO: *No.*
FLEA ONE: *So I must have misunderstood and—*
FLEA TWO: *Yes.*
FLEA ONE: *And you don't think it's a dumb dream—*
FLEA TWO: *No.*
FLEA ONE: *And you want to—*
FLEA TWO: *Yes.*
FLEA ONE: *Join the circus with me—*
FLEA TWO: *No.*
FLEA ONE: *Well, that's just fantas—um . . . did you just say NO?*
FLEA TWO: *Yes.*

Interruption!

We interrupt our regularly scheduled fleas for a special report on interrupting—to find out when it's rude and when it's not.

EXTREMELY RUDE	NOT VERY RUDE
Example 1: "Who cut!"	Example 1: "What is that peculiar odor? Oh, hello, Grandma!"
Example 2: "Barferoni!"	Example 2: "Excuse me, but a slimy worm is dangling out of your mouth!"
Example 3: "Shut up!"	Example 3: "Shhh, I believe I hear an ugly polka-dot monster sneaking up behind you!"
Example 4: "I said shut up!"	Example 4: "Please be quiet; he's playing my favorite song on the accordion!"

FLEA ONE: *But—*

FLEA TWO: *No, I DON'T want to join the circus! I'm scared of heights, remember? I'm a chicken, remember? Cluck cluck. No, I don't want to JOIN the circus!*

FLEA ONE: *I'm afraid I don't underst—*

FLEA TWO: *I want to help YOU join the circus!*

FLEA ONE: *Oh . . . I get it. . . .*

FLEA TWO: *Sure! I'll hold the hoop while you jump through it. I'll stand under the trapeze and catch you if you fall. I'll stuff you into a cannon. I'll keep the chain saws oiled . . . whatever.*

FLEA ONE: *Wow . . . that's just great. . . . Thanks!*

Flea One was so excited he almost forgot to ask one last question.

FLEA ONE: *Why?*
FLEA TWO: *Because you're the one who has a dream to believe in.*

Meanwhile

Barry finally moved a muscle; to be specific, one of his eyelids twitched.

18

One giant leap

This hurts like all get-out was Barry's first and only wobbly thought as he began to stir. He winced in pain as he gingerly squinted through the tiny slits of his eyelids, beyond the blurry mesh of eyelashes, and out onto the vast, shapeless morning whiteness of the hospital room ceiling.

Barry had no idea where he was, if anywhere. He opened his eyes a little wider and the brightness stung his eyes. The ceiling still looked entirely like nothing to him: a big empty sky of nothing.

A large cloud drifted across the sky and into view overhead. The cloud spoke softly:

"Barry . . . ? Sweetie . . . ? Are you awake . . . ? It's me, Mom. Can you hear me?"

Barry couldn't answer even if he wanted to because of his dry throat, because he was a boyhound, and because he was swaddled up like an ancient dead pharaoh. That'll usually do it.

So Barry just blinked and blinked, hoping this would somehow transmit a message to his mom, as if his blinking were a secret code* she might somehow understand. Here is what Barry's blinking and blinking was trying to say, although not in these exact words:

1. Boy, does it ever hurt like all get-out.
2. Boy, am I ever glad you're here, Mom.
3. And Janey too . . . honest.
4. Where the heck am I?
5. And how, exactly, the heck did I get here?

*Samuel Morse invented both the telegraph and Morse code—a system of dots and dashes for each letter. But before becoming a pioneer of electromagnetics, he was quite a famous painter, and once he ran for mayor of New York City. He didn't win, though.

Of course, Mrs. Barry's Mom—being a mom, and being better than Santa Claus in many regards—had no problem understanding Barry's Special Blink Code.

***

Moms can be so scary, the way they know everything. Good thing they're on your side, mostly.

***

She told Barry about Pierre and the crab apple tree, about the car that was going maybe a little too fast, about the ambulance with the screaming siren, about the tests and the X-rays, about the mummy and the drawbridge.

Of course, Barry—being a boyhound—did not understand a word. But from the gentle, sorry way Mrs. Barry's Mom spoke, Barry's boyhound instinct knew two things: that everything was going to be pretty much okay, sooner or later, and that everything was pretty much all his fault.

Tower Bridge is one of the world's most famous drawbridges. It raises and lowers three or four times every day to let tall ships sail along the River Thames (***TEMS***). People sometimes confuse it with London Bridge—a different bridge entirely, and not a drawbridge either.

While Barry listened, Janey kept inching closer to her mom and closer to Barry. In her hands she held what was left of Pierre: a tangle of long red woolly string attached with gobs and gobs of nearly dry glue to a torn cardboard box that had once contained macaroni and a pouch of cheese powder.

Barry turned his head slowly, painfully, an

inch or two, just enough to see his sister standing timidly at the side of his bed. Janey clutched Partial Pierre more tightly to her chest and looked at Barry.

Barry shifted his eyes to look down toward the mangled marionette, then back up to Janey. He blinked one long sorry blink at her.

"That's okay," said Janey, who I bet will become somebody's mom someday. "It was no big fat disaster."

Bang! went the door to Barry's hospital room.

Well, okay, maybe it didn't go *bang!* exactly, but it did seem especially loud because everything had been so quiet and whispery up till now. Sort of like when you're just drifting off to sleep, and then the person on the top bunk starts snoring, for Pete's sake.

To tell you the truth, the door actually sounded more like this: *shh-kung*—with no exclamation mark.

It was a nurse who shh-kunged the door open, and she pushed a trolley loaded with rattly nurse stuff to the far side of Barry's bed.

"Good morning," she sang out to everyone. Then to Barry she said, "Oh, good, you're awake, it's time for your medicine, here you go, open wide."

Barry didn't understand a word she said, and he couldn't open his mouth exactly what you'd call "wide," so the nurse carefully placed a pill on Barry's tongue, then gave him a couple swallows of cold water.

The nurse was chatty and nice and smelled like flowery soap. She explained a few things to Barry as she held up a thermometer from her trolley; Barry hoped very much that it wasn't the kind of thermometer that goes up your rhymes-with-conundrum.*

*__ka-*NUN*-drum__ A difficult problem or situation, such as "I'm having trouble finding a polite word that rhymes with *bum*."

"We're going to take your temperature, then we'll take a peek under those bandages and see how you're coming along," said the nurse. "You've had quite the adventure, young man." She glanced at his leg cast, then reached over and lightly rapped a knuckle on the hard plaster drawbridge over the peaceful White Sheets River, so to speak. Then, very much to Barry's relief, she slid the thermometer under his tongue.

***

I'm afraid you'll have to hang on a minute or two here. Waiting for a thermometer is like toasting a strawberry Pop-Tart: it's boring, but there's no point in taking it out till it's done. I do apologize.

***

While she was waiting, the nurse sat on the edge of Barry's bed and eased her finger ever so gently under the bandages around Barry's head and lifted them a tiny bit. Then she leaned in really close for a glimpse of his mushy old papaya.

Just to let you know: Barry did not smell like nice flowery soap.

Up there on Barry's head

Flea Two was so excited he was rocking back and forth and from side to side as if he were a basketball player trying to deke Flea One and go in for the easy layup. Except that Flea Two also had a huge silly grin on his face, and basketball players usually look all serious and stuff when they're trying to score on you.

For some reason Flea One still did not seem entirely

Basketball was invented by a YMCA gym teacher simply to give athletes exercise in the winter. Now it's a major sport even when it's nice out.

sure about all this. He was skeptical. It all seemed too good to be true. Fleas are like people. Nothing makes them more confused than giving them exactly what they ask for.

So Flea One and Flea Two just kind of looked back and forth into each other's eyes for like a month:

FLEA TWO'S LOOK: [Huge silly grin: *C'mon!*]
FLEA ONE'S LOOK: [Squinty sideways glance: *I'm not entirely sure about all this.*]
FLEA TWO'S LOOK: [Even huger silly grin: *And why not?*]
FLEA ONE'S LOOK: [Squinty scowl: *This better not be some kind of joke. I'm warning you.*]
FLEA TWO'S LOOK: [Big huge incredibly silly grin: *Nope. Not joking.*]
FLEA ONE'S LOOK: [Squinty sideways scowl: *Well, I dunno.*]
FLEA TWO'S LOOK: [Big large huge stupendously silly grin: *Trust me.*]
FLEA ONE'S LOOK: [Sideways squint: *You seem sincere, and yet I can't help but wonder.*]
FLEA TWO'S LOOK: [Scowl: *That's enough. This grin is starting to hurt.*]

Flea Two could see he wasn't getting anywhere by just making faces at Flea One. He was going to have to say actual real words right out loud to prove that he was serious, *to get through* to Flea One.

FLEA TWO: *Let me get this straight. You want to join the circus, right?*
FLEA ONE: *Yeah.*
FLEA TWO: *So what's the holdup? Let's go.*
FLEA ONE: *You sure?*
FLEA TWO: *I'm sure. Now take my hand . . . no, the other hand . . . that's right.*
FLEA ONE: *Okay, let's blow this Popsicle stand.*
FLEA TWO: *Yeah, let's cheese it. This is a funny-tasting dog anyway.*

Flea One and Flea Two joined hands, aimed for the small opening in Barry's bandages where the light shone through, and in one giant leap they sprang off Barry's head and into new uncharted territory.

FLEA ONE AND FLEA TWO: *Geronimoooooooooooooooo!!!**

Meanwhile

All at once the nurse felt a mysterious itching on top of her head. She immediately sat up straight—she *bolted upright,* as they say—as if someone had stuffed ice cubes down the back of her uniform. She looked quickly left, then quickly right, then quickly left again, with a startled look on her face, like a jittery prairie dog searching the wild blue yonder for swooping eagles.

The nurse slid off the edge of Barry's bed and slumped onto the floor. She stayed crouched down there for nearly a whole minute as if she were looking for something tiny and fragile she had dropped, or had just noticed how groovy the geometric floor tiles looked from that angle.

***je-RON-na-mo** Geronimo was a fearless Apache medicine man who led the very last Native American fighting force to surrender to the United States. They thought he had magic powers because he was so hard to capture. Today people yell *Geronimo!* when they do stupid, dangerous things, in hopes that some of his magic will rub off. (It never does.)

Mrs. Barry's Mom and Janey stood on the other side of the bed, looking at each other, completely puzzled, totally bemused, entirely befuddled. Neither of them could think of a single thing to say.

Barry the Drawbridge Mummy couldn't see much of anything. He couldn't move very much either. He was pretty much stuck there on top of the bed.

Mrs. Barry's Mom wondered if maybe she ought to call for help or something, to go get a nurse for the nurse.

Just as she decided that yes, she ought to call for help, the nurse suddenly jumped up—she actually jumped right up into the air, quite high for a nurse—and she *howled.*

It was quite loud too. It sounded exactly like this:

"Owww-oooooooh!!!"

It truly does deserve three exclamation marks.

Then she did it again, I guess in case anybody missed it the first time:

"Ow Ow Ow-ooooooooh!!!"

Janey held Partial Pierre tight as the nurse rushed past her and ran from the room, howling and howling, as fast as anybody can possibly run wearing those sensible white nurse shoes.

***

They ought to put her picture in *The Guinness Book of World Records*. Right next to the Jiffy Pop raccoon.

***

That is when Barry suddenly spoke. "Sheesh! What's all the racket?" he said right out loud in English just before the door went *bang!*—yes, it actually did go *bang!* this time. Mrs. Barry's Mom stared at Barry, then at the door, then back at Barry.

"What was that, sweetie?" said Mrs. Barry's Mom, leaning in closer to hear him. "Did you say something?"

"I think he said, 'Sheep are tall as rabbits,'" said Janey with a shrug and a frown.

"Hmm," said Mrs. Barry's Mom doubtfully.

Remember: those were the first human words Barry had spoken in a long, long time, and with his bandaged-up mummy mouth, all he could do was mumble.

"Lost my toys," said Barry—or so it sounded—although he actually said, "Lots of noise."

Mrs. Barry's Mom slowly shook her head at Barry's nonsense. "Poor thing, he got quite a nasty bump on the head. We'd better let him rest." Mrs. Barry's Mom and Janey sat quietly on the visitors' chairs, leaving Barry to stare straight up into the vast, shapeless nothing of the ceiling.

***

Just to let you know: Mrs. Barry's Mom

secretly knew exactly what Barry was saying. You know what moms are like. She also knew that just taking a deep breath to speak must hurt Barry like all get-out. She knew that he really needed his rest right now.

***

No offense to the nice flowery-soap nurse, but Barry was glad to be alone with his mom and sister—glad about this for maybe the first time in the entire History of the Universe.

The moment the fleas jumped off Barry's head and the nurse ran screaming, Barry's boy brain had woken up all of a sudden like magic. But his boy memory was still foggy and groggy—it was just groaning out of bed in flannel cowboy pajamas, so to speak. It was trying to make sense of his boyhound day like a dream that slips further away with every moment of wakefulness. According to Barry's memory, there was a werewolf elevator, a butterscotch worm, Vladimir Guerrero's pants, a flowery frog, two crunchy squirrel sandwiches, a lumpy cat lamp, and a macaroni-and-glue dinner.*

Barry's brain could easily tell these were not dreams, that it was all true in some strange way, just not exactly the way his memory seemed to remember.

With all these out-of-focus memories playing like an old silent movie in his head, Barry realized he had a million things to say, a million things to ask, and a million things to say sorry for. But the time would come. It's never too late, especially to apologize. On the other hand, when your father is coming home tomorrow, and you'll probably have to suffer through all 7 Dadly Sins, an apology can never come too soon either. *Good thinking,* thought Barry to himself, in those exact words.

As much as it hurt to speak, there was

*See APPENDIX VI for a timeline of Barry's actual boyhound day.

something he needed to say to his mom. Barry took a deep, painful breath. "Moon?"

"Yes, sweetie?" said Mrs. Barry's Mom, rising from her chair to go to Barry's bedside.

"Eye apollo jive," mumbled Barry.

"Never mind," said Mrs. Barry's Mom. "The important thing is that you're going to be okay."

"Things for bean hair," said the mummy mouth.

"You're welcome," said Mrs. Barry's Mom. "And I'll stay here until you're all better. But you need to be quiet and rest now, okay?" Barry nodded ever so slightly, just enough for Mrs. Barry's Mom to see.

Still, there was something more happening deep inside his mushy old papaya. Little by little, slowly but surely as a sunrise, Barry's brain was filling up with new stuff about what it means to be a boy, and this feeling made Barry totally relaxed.

And peaceful.

And happy.

And so on.

Looking straight up into the big white nothing, he couldn't see his mom and Janey, but he knew they were there. Then somewhere under the bandages, even though it hurt a little, Barry's mummy mouth grew into a slow smile—but only Barry knew it was there.

***

When they make this into a movie, this is when they'll play a bunch of nice music with probably violins or whatever to try to make everybody cry because it's a happy ending and stuff like that.

On the other hand, because Barry has learned something from all this, since everything has turned out okay, a more "triumphant" piece might be suitable, say, the theme music from the first *Rocky* movie, but we'd have to ask permission. Or even "Smoke on the Water."* I mean, why not? A lot of people tend to like that song.

***

As I mentioned, Barry was feeling very relaxed, warmed by the gentle sunrise dawning across the misty landscape of his fertile mind. You just be quiet: I *know* it's a schnooky metaphor; the violins must be getting to me. I do apologize.

For a while now, Barry's boy brain had been oozing back in, like maple syrup soaking into a big spongy warm waffle until every last crumb becomes heavy with sweetness and goo. At first this made Barry think quite a lot about his mom, his dad, and even his sister. Maybe it wasn't for the first time in the History of the Universe, but it was certainly the first time in a long time.

*Deep Purple was a rock group popular in the 1970s, when "Smoke on the Water" was a big hit. Other good British groups are Pink Floyd, Led Zeppelin, The Who, Jethro Tull, T. Rex, and Queen.

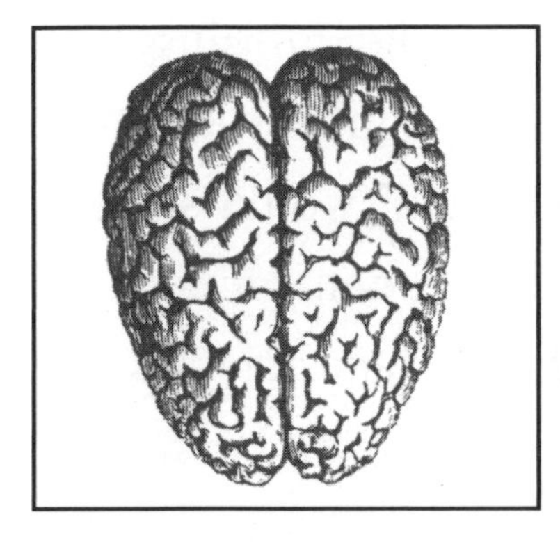

Barry's actual brain.

Barry's metaphorical brain.

Not all his memories would return completely, however. Which was probably a good thing. Sometimes when your mind won't let you remember stuff—especially bad stuff—it's just trying to do you a favor so you don't go crazy and wind up living in the furnace room wearing pajamas and a cowboy hat for the rest of your life. That's why most of the actual details of what happened during Barry's boyhound day remained unclear to him, and I hope they always will.

Barry knew that his memory was fuzzy,

that there were large chunks missing altogether, but the little he could remember seemed pretty cool. Just like it would seem to a boy. And just like a boy, soon enough his thoughts turned to his two best friends, the Brothers. *Wait till I tell them all this weird stuff,* thought Barry. And then, *Naw, forget it, they'd never believe me.*

epilogue

An epilogue is a sort of extra chapter at the end of a book where they blab on about extra stuff after the story is officially finished.

Take a mystery novel. In the last chapter the detective leans against the fireplace and explains to everyone in the mansion how he investigated all the clues and all the suspects and figured out who the heck the murderer was—how he knew *whodunnit*—and everybody gasps in surprise and then it's over.*

*Agatha Christie is the most famous writer of mystery stories in the world. She wrote *Death on the Nile* and *The Mousetrap,* among many others. She lived to be eighty-five years old. And no, in case you were wondering, she wasn't murdered.

In the epilogue you find out how the evildoers get their *comeuppance,* how the innocent citizens return to their regular poison-free lives, and how the events of the story affected everybody and whether they get to live happily ever after or not.

That's the thing with stories in a book or on TV or whatever: they have to start somewhere and they have to end somewhere and in the middle there's all the stuff in the middle.

Real stories are entirely not like that. Real stories are the ones that have actually happened to you, the ones that are *always* happening, the ones always rattling around up there inside your big human brain. These stories—call them experiences, or memories, if you like—don't always have any particular beginning, middle, or end. Most stuff just happens whenever it feels like happening, and there's never a handy epilogue at the end to explain everything.

Still, it might be kind of fun to pretend that the story in a book can go on forever too, even though everybody knows it isn't actually true.

In case you're interested, here is the epilogue to this particular not-real story. This is what happens in the future to the characters—the dramatis personae—in their order of appearance, only because I couldn't think of any better order to put them in.

Barry

I'm delighted to report from the future that Barry was pretty much okay after they unraveled his bandages and took the cast off his leg. But if you held your breath and squinted, you could pretty much see that Barry walked with a slight limp. Plus he got headaches more than most other people, and for some reason he could never stand the taste of papaya. He never ate another peanut butter sandwich either. Barry also suffered from a rare case of geppettophobia* and had to see a specialist until he was

***jeh-*PET*-oh-*FO*-bee-ah** Named after Geppetto, the fictional wood carver who made Pinocchio, geppettophobia is the mysterious fear of puppets, marionettes, and anything with strings attached. Geppettophobia is not real as far as I know. I just made it up.

twenty-eight years old. It so happens that turning into a boyhound overnight like magic was not the strangest thing that would ever happen to Barry, but I am not at liberty to discuss any details at this particular time. Otherwise Barry was just fine.

Flea One and Flea Two

I'm delighted to report from the future that these two fellows indeed became a howling success, so to speak, in the circus. After a number of setbacks involving incorrect amounts of gunpowder, Flea One perfected the art of being fired out of a cannon, astonishing audiences far and wide as the Great Flealini. When his popularity as a performer began to fade, he developed a range of organic blood-flavored pasta sauces—for example, Chunky Scab with Real Dandruff Flakes—plus a series of step-by-step exercise videos. As the Great Flealini's manager and partner, Flea Two became one of the greatest impresarios in the entire animal kingdom. They eventually retired in Florida on top of a nice comfortable Labrador retriever, and although they continued to argue pretty much every day, they remained the best of friends until the end.

The Brothers

I'm delighted to report from the future that, despite everything, Barry and the Brothers remained best friends.

Sometimes boys are like boyhounds: they forget stuff almost as fast as it happens. After all, the slower, bitten Brother was just fine after a nice teacher cleaned his leg and put on three big square Band-Aids. I mean, it's not like Barry had rabies or anything. That Brother grew up and became a doctor with *Médecins sans Frontières* (**mayd-*SAN* sohn *FRONTY*-air**), an organization that has won the Nobel Prize for bringing humanitarian aid to people suffering from wars, disease, famine, and other disasters. The faster, unbitten Brother became a history professor specializing in the map-making, or cartography (**kar-*TOG*-ra-fee**), of the War of 1812.

Exploding Raccoon

Well, as you know, the raccoon exploded, and that, as they say, is that.

Janey

I'm delighted to report from the future that Janey continued to be a very normal sister, a very normal girl, a very normal person. Soon enough—*too* soon, if you ask her mother—Janey had plenty of smoochy boyfriend secrets to write in her book that nobody is allowed to read. If you ask Janey now, she'll say she wants to be a doctor when she grows up. Please don't tell her I said this, but Janey will actually become quite a well-known artist and musician. One of these days you will be able to hear some of her songs on the radio.

Mrs. Barry's Mom

I'm delighted to report from the future that Mrs. Barry's Mom never found out that Barry turned into a boyhound—by the way, thanks for not telling her—well, she didn't find out *exactly,* anyway. One day, after someone let the cat out by accident and it came back filthy the next morning, Mrs. Barry's Mom felt a peculiar itching on her head and had a sudden urge to drink milk out of a bowl with her tongue. Then she ate a quarter pound of pimento loaf without unwrapping it from the waxy paper. This odd momcat sensation lasted about half an hour, and luckily no one else was home at the time. From that day on, Mrs. Barry's Mom never jumped to any conclusions about other people's behavior, particularly Barry's. And she was always a great mom, and better than Santa Claus in many regards.

Worm

Let's not get into disgusting details about what happens to you when you get swallowed, okay? Let's just say we all have a pretty good idea of what became of the worm and leave it at that.

I'm With Stupid

I'm delighted to report from the future that I'm With Stupid got tired of being in a band that only played songs from Canadian power-rock trios, even though his hair was perfect for it. Instead he became a men's fashion designer and made tight pants popular again for maybe six months.

Vladimir Guerrero

I'm delighted to report from the future that Vladimir Guerrero the dog soon settled down on a nice oval rug with a nice French poodle named Marie and they raised eight cute little woolly poodlets together. Meanwhile, Vladimir Guerrero the human continues to be one of the great baseball players of his generation.

Squashed Frog

Well, as you know, the frog was torn to bits, and that, as they say, is that.

Monica and 19 Other Squirrels

I'm delighted to report from the future that Monica became violently ill from too much peanut butter after the attack on Barry and vowed never again to jump on any animal that didn't even know what kind of animal it was. The 19 other squirrels all got sick too. But they never learned their lesson. One week after the attack on Barry, the final fat squirrel traded Barry's tattered knapsack to some hikers for half a jar of Skippy.

Cat

I'm delighted to report from the future that the cat was copacetic when Barry came home from the hospital, and her instinct told her Barry was normal again, so it was okay to come out from behind the furnace. Barry still always forgot to clean out her litter box even though one year the cat gave him a new spatula for his birthday.

Pierre/Partial Pierre

After Pierre became Partial, after the accident, after they came home from visiting Barry in the hospital, Janey placed the scraggly remains of the marionette on a shelf in her closet, where she kept him as a sad dusty souvenir of the day Something Truly Awful happened. Then one Tuesday afternoon years later, when Janey had gone to school, a new cleaning lady came in and just threw him away with the garbage.

Driver of Car

I'm delighted to report from the future that he didn't drive fast anymore. In fact, after the accident he vowed to never drive his car again. He traded it in for a bright yellow motor scooter that he rode all year—even in winter—very, very slowly, dressed in bright yellow overalls with a matching helmet. He never found out that his neighbors secretly called him the Caterpillar behind his back.

Nurse

I'm delighted to report from the future that eventually she was okay. But it took a while. Because, if you remember, she ran howling from the hospital room. Then she ran howling from the entire hospital and was not heard from again for three months, when her sister received a postcard from Florida. She then moved to Winnipeg and married a man who had tattoos over his entire body.

APPENDIX I

COMPLEAT PIRATE

OBJECT OF GAME

The object of Pirate is to win before the other team does.

NO GUFF, BUT HOW?

Just cool your jets. You have to read all the rules first.

RULES

1.1 Read all the rules.

2.1 No cheating.

2.2 Unless of course the other team cheats first.

3.1 Decide on a treasure. It should be small enough to carry but large enough to find. A box would be great. For example, a breadbox, toolbox, jewelry box (remove bread, tools, jewelry, especially if you never asked permission to borrow it in the first place).

3.2 Put stuff like gum or a pack of cards or whatever in the box for loot.

3.3 Make sure everybody gets a good look at the treasure.

3.4 Decide on how much time is allowed to hide the treasure.

4.1 One team hides the treasure, and the other team can't peek.

4.2	The team that hides the treasure has to draw a good map.
4.3	Lousy maps are not allowed: that's just cheating.
4.4	Put which way is north on the map, or that's usually cheating too.
5.1	Decide on how many Mississippis the other team gets to find the treasure, or just pick a time like three o'clock or whatever, then just time it with your watch.
5.2	Up to 99 bonus Mississippis may be given for a head start in case the treasure is hard to find or your map is a bit lousy.
6.1	Hints and clues just wreck the game.
6.2	Once the game begins everybody must always speak in their best Pirate voice. All sentences must end with "matey" or "me hearties."
6.3	When the team looking for the treasure thinks they have found it, they must yell "arrgh" real loud so everybody can hear it and come see.
7.1	If the team looking for the treasure finds it before time's up, then they win, otherwise the team that hid the treasure wins.
7.2	The winning team keeps all the loot (gum, cards, money, whatever) and they don't have to share it if they don't feel like it.
7.3	Remember to put the treasure box back exactly where you borrowed it from.

APPENDIX II

PEANUT BUTTER SANDWICHES

by master chef Andrea di Lancia

an-*DRAY*-ah dih *LAN*-see-ah Andrea di Lancia is a special name I use for writing cookbooks. It is nearly Italian for Andy Spearman, and everybody knows the best chefs are always Italian whenever they're not French. These are all real peanut butter sandwiches that taste good if you ask me. I am delighted to share them with you now.

The Ski Slope

Place 2 bread slices faceup on preparation surface. On 1 slice spread a thick, even coat of crunchy peanut butter. It must be crunchy, as this represents the rugged landscape for which this sandwich is named. Set aside. On the other slice spread a thick layer of Hellmann's real mayonnaise, representing snow. Flip the second slice onto the first, so that the "snow" falls onto the "mountain." Eat. A crisp, tangy, outdoorsy flavor. Serve with chilled spring water.

The Astroturf

Place 1 bread slice faceup on preparation surface. Spread a perfectly even layer of smooth peanut butter. Position 1 flat leaf of iceberg lettuce on top to create turf top. Trim lettuce to edge of crust. Dot with raisins to create baseball diamond, or squeeze mayo or mustard in careful lines for football grid. Do not cut. Add second bread slice for a domed stadium if desired. Eat. An invigorating, athletic choice. Serve with Gatorade.

The Frog 'n' Mud

Place 2 bread slices faceup on preparation surface. On 1 slice spread a very thick layer of peanut butter. Microwave till gooey. Remove from microwave. Slice one large dill pickle in half lengthwise. Squish pickle into peanut butter mud, frog side up. Place other bread slice on top. Slice. Eat. A hot, swampy, runny treat. Serve with chocolate milk and plenty of napkins.

The Quattro Frutti (4 Fruits)

Place 2 bread slices faceup on preparation surface. On 1 slice spread a layer of peanut butter. Set aside. On the other slice carefully apply 4 different fruit jams, including marmalade if desired, each occupying one-quarter of bread surface. Place first slice on top. Cut into quarters. Eat. A classic European creation. Serve with San Pellegrino lemon-lime soda and a straw.

The Mount Etna

Place 1 bread slice faceup on preparation surface. Spread a thick layer of crunchy peanut butter on top. Place as many slices of cheddar cheese as possible on the peanut butter. Microwave till cheese bubbles like a Sicilian volcano and peanut butter oozes like molten magma. Eat carefully with knife and fork. A hot, lava-like sandwich. Serve with milk.

APPENDIX III

A Sample Boyhound Dream

Barry kept sinking in a huge bowl of quicksand popcorn shaped like tiny raccoons. An exploding voice called out—a one-legged frog waiting for the bus. Atta boy, fetch the stick, said the polka-dot voice of a wet tennis poodle. The wheezing accordion stumbled down the crunchy peanut butter staircase and swarmed a red lollipop blanket, hiding socks escaping from the wet laundry jail. The strawberry shoe box took the elevator while it rained angry lobsters. Barry's sweatshirt interrupted like a lame Halloween knapsack. Then on the mushy papaya moon the bingo boat sank like a final squirrel. Everybody waited for the Pop-Tart parade before throwing Mississippi bones into the dumbest Stanley Cup in the world. A pair of pirates zoomed in on magic pineapple carpets. The pirates turned into Mrs. Barry's Mom, drifting away like a macaroni mummy. Somebody silently farted, and a crafty old woman appeared, opening a powdered hand, knuckles unfurling like petals of a rusty flower, skin crackled like crushed eggshells. Good doggie, want some yummy raisins? Hundreds of little white raisins squirmed in her open palm. Then Elvis woke up the werewolf and it was all a dream.

APPENDIX IV

Dear Diary,

Barry said a bad word today,

he called you stupid diarrhea.

your secret best friend,

Janey

APPENDIX V

I really shouldn't be telling you this, but okay, I'll tell you about the time Barry peed in his snowsuit if you promise to keep it under your hat. It happened on a dare. Well, nobody actually said, "Barry, I dare you to pee in your snowsuit." There weren't many dares Barry wouldn't do, but that is probably one of them. (On second thought, you never know.) Anyway, last winter, the Saturday after the biggest blizzard since the Pleistocene epoch,* it was minus eight billion degrees out, and Barry and the Brothers were building a snow fort. When they finished, they found out that only two of them could actually fit inside, so Barry, who so happened to not be one of the Brothers, was told to stand outside, to stand on guard and warn them in case of invaders or girls. Barry knew from experience that you can't fight two brothers at the same time and win. This wouldn't have

PLY-sto-seen EP-uck An epoch is a period of time lasting hundreds of thousands of years, for example the Math Class epoch. The Pleistocene ended ten thousand years ago, when the Ice Age ended and everyone could finally put their shorts back on.

been such a big fat deal if Barry got to hold a machine gun or at least a big twig that maybe looked like a machine gun from a distance. But all the cool sticks were buried under two feet of snow, so Barry got mad.

"I don't need to go inside a stupid fort," Barry shouted. "It's perfectly warm out here. I could stand out here all day."

That's when the older Brother poked his head out of the fort and dared Barry to do exactly that.

Hours later, when it was getting dark, Barry was still standing there, since the dare was still in effect even though the Brothers had already gone home by then. Barry couldn't hold it in any longer. At first the wet trickle spread warmly down the inside of his leg, and Barry almost fainted with relief. But within, say, one minute, the pee began to freeze and Barry felt even colder than before, and then he had to hobble all the way home in a snowsuit with one pretty stiff leg.

APPENDIX VI

A Boyhound Timeline

Here is a general guide to Barry's boyhound day.
The times are as near as I can remember.
I mean, please, I didn't exactly use a stopwatch.
You may also notice that it covers pretty much
a twenty-four-hour period from the time he woke up
Monday morning to the time the fleas abandoned ship.

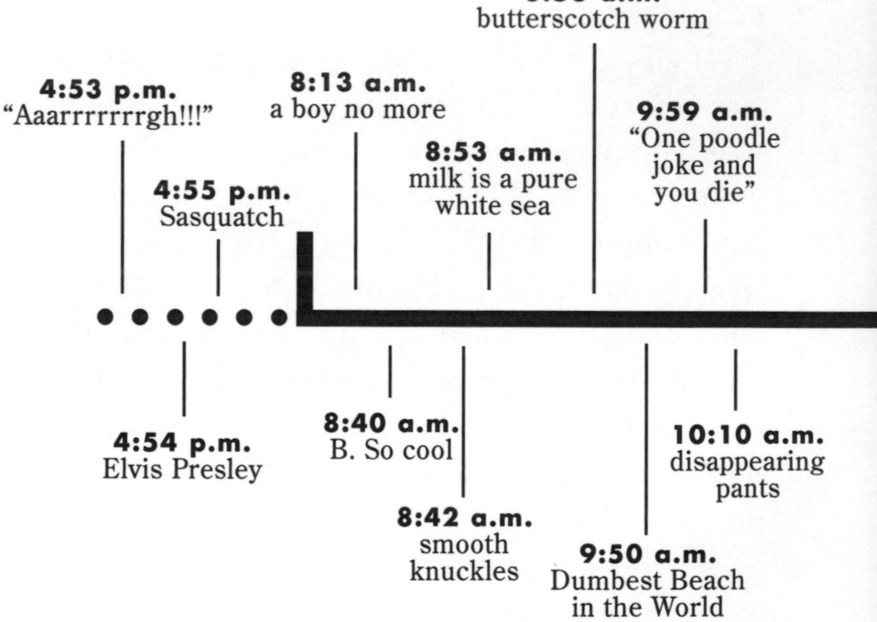

MONDAY

10:41 a.m.
convenient fire hydrant

10:59 a.m.
Sniff the Frog

11:18 a.m.
pot roast or half a dozen turnips

Noon
a familiar clanging sound

12:08 p.m.
lame Halloween costume

12:15 p.m.
Get him, girls!

12:32 p.m.
poor little innocent dead frog

12:45 p.m.
tackle

12:47 p.m.
winning the Stanley Cup

12:52 p.m.
stupidly happy

1:00 p.m.
peekaboo with a coffee cup

1:02 p.m.
The 5 Phases of Upset Mothers

MONDAY

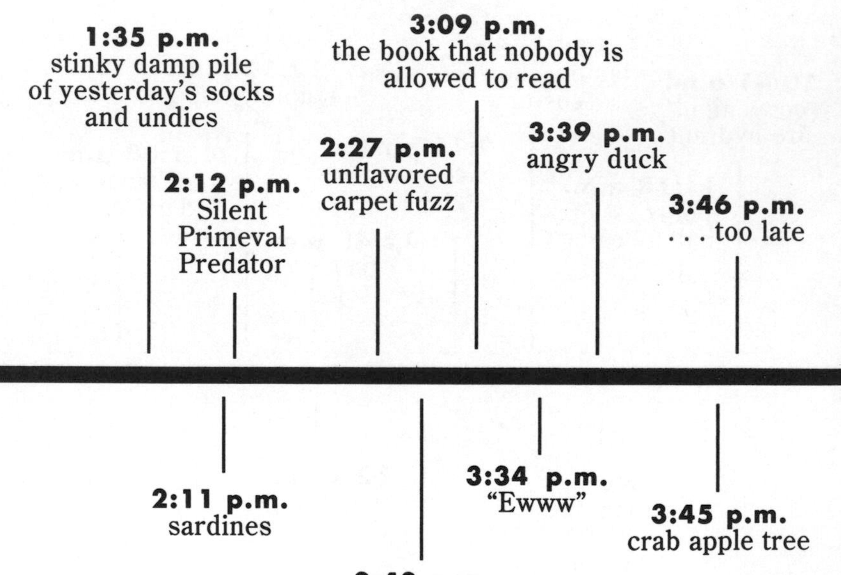
1:35 p.m.
stinky damp pile of yesterday's socks and undies
2:11 p.m.
sardines
2:12 p.m.
Silent Primeval Predator
2:27 p.m.
unflavored carpet fuzz
2:40 p.m.
$x \leq [(a - b) \div \Delta c] \bullet \pi r^2$
3:09 p.m.
the book that nobody is allowed to read
3:34 p.m.
"Ewww"
3:39 p.m.
angry duck
3:45 p.m.
crab apple tree
3:46 p.m.
. . . too late

TUESDAY

7:51 a.m.
the talking cloud

7:54 a.m.
the drawbridge mummy

8:10 a.m.
rhymes with conundrum

8:13 a.m.
"Geronimo!"

8:19 a.m.
"Smoke on the Water"

8:22 a.m.
spongy warm waffle

index

Animals and creatures

Contraptions, inventions, and stuff

Etymology (word origins)

Ingestibles—food and related items

Places, real and imagined

Science and math